Arid Dreams

STORIES

Duanwad Pimwana

Translated from the Thai
by Mui Poopoksakul

FEMINIST
PRESS
AT THE CITY UNIVERSITY
OF NEW YORK
NEW YORK CITY

Published in 2019 by the Feminist Press
at the City University of New York
The Graduate Center
365 Fifth Avenue, Suite 5406
New York, NY 10016

feministpress.org

First Feminist Press edition 2019

The stories in *Arid Dreams* were originally published in Thailand in the collections
หนังสือเล่มสอง (1995), แดดสิบแปดนาฬิกา (2006), สัมพันธภาพ (2006), and ฝันแห้ง
และเรื่องอื่นๆ (2014). "Sandals" was first published in the magazine กรุงเทพธุรกิจ
(*Bangkok Business*) in 2000.

 This book was made possible thanks to a grant from New
York State Council on the Arts with the support of Governor
Andrew M. Cuomo and the New York State Legislature.

This book is supported in part by an award from the National Endowment
for the Arts.

First printing April 2019

Cover design by Suki Boynton
Text design by Drew Stevens

Library of Congress Cataloging-in-Publication Data is available for this title.

CONTENTS

ARID DREAMS

I'D WAITED TOO LONG TO COME BACK. THIS PLACE USED
to be my dream vacation spot back when I was a student,
but now it bore so little resemblance to its former self
that I had to question my memory. There wasn't a single room available to rent, no matter how good or terrible the location. On the beach the sun was so bright it
hurt my eyes, and people, their skin reddish, whitish,
had distributed themselves densely on the sand and in
the water. The restaurants and bars were packed. The
ocean breeze was stifled by the long line of umbrellas
and nylon beach chairs that were squeezed together.
There were some tents with rows of beds set up underneath and young female masseuses in smart uniforms
stationed nearby, beckoning to tourists.

I forged ahead, stopping frequently to inquire about
a place to stay. If I'd wanted to camp on the beach, there
were still some tents available for rent, but as far as I
could see, the areas where you could pitch them were
far below my standards. Finding myself more and more
disheartened, I felt the urge to hop back on the boat and
return to the mainland. It was so crowded that even if I
managed to find a place to stay . . . A vacation where you

had to fight for every single thing? I was exhausted just thinking about it.

The crowd eventually started to thin out toward the end of the beach. The sand had given way to craggy rocks covered in algae. Seeing only a fishing village beyond, I stopped walking. The beach was beginning to turn into a marsh anyway: all black mud and red mangrove stilts. As I turned to head back, I suddenly came face-to-face with a short, dark-skinned man. He smiled, showing off a mouthful of white teeth, as if he were actually happy to see me.

"You're looking for a place to stay, right, *hia*? There aren't any around here. You've got to go farther inland." The man pointed toward the fishing village. "Come and have a look." He signaled, leading the way, but I hesitated because I'd already decided to go back to the mainland. "You can have a look first. It's only six hundred baht a night, unlimited water and electricity. There's even a kitchen, in case you don't feel like walking to the beachfront. Come! There's only one room left."

I started to follow him, but stayed on my guard. I didn't trust these shady-looking vendors on the beach. This one wasn't wearing a shirt, only gray fisherman's pants and dark blue flip-flops. Along the way, I took note of my surroundings: rows of homes built close together. We were quite far from the beach by this point, and there was still no sign of bungalows or other accommodations for rent. I got increasingly anxious and kept asking when we would arrive; we'd wandered some distance from anything remotely resembling a tourist area. The short man kept insisting, just a little farther, just a little farther, but we kept walking. I became even more alert. Eventually, I refused to continue walking because I thought we'd gone too far. When I stopped, he did, too.

"Here we are." He'd stopped in front of a wooden house elevated waist-high. It had a large porch and looked like it had two or three bedrooms. "Go right up. I'll take you to see the rooms." He rinsed his feet with water from an earthen jar at the foot of the stairs before leading me into the house.

I felt uneasy. There was nothing to indicate that tourists could stay here; it felt more like I was visiting relatives in the country. You couldn't hear the waves, there was no view, and the decor left much to be desired, but the room that he showed me looked tolerable. I wondered if I should give it a go for a night and head back tomorrow—what could be the harm in that? I felt like I could use a massage, so it probably wouldn't hurt to get a room, walk back to the waterfront, and hire one of those girls for an hour or two. If I found a masseuse with skilled hands and a nice personality, I might even change my mind and extend my stay for a few more nights.

Signaling that the room was satisfactory, I agreed to stay for one night and paid in cash. The short man, who by the looks of things was the owner, handed me the keys and explained, "There are two keys, sir. The little one is for the room. The big one is for the house—sometimes when we're all out, we lock the front door, too. Please help yourself to anything in the house. Feel free to make yourself coffee and watch TV in the common area, but if you want to order food from the kitchen, you have to see if the cook's in. She's usually here in the afternoon . . . The bathroom's this way. You have to walk through the kitchen here and go down the stairs at the back. There, that's the bathroom. There's one stall for the toilet and one for the shower. You can also shower on the little cement landing in front of the bathroom. I've installed a showerhead, do you see it? That's it. Make yourself at home. But are you sure you're just staying one night, so I'll let other guests book for tomorrow?"

Once he'd wrapped up the tour, the owner of the guesthouse left me alone. As I was walking back to my room, I heard him calling somebody named Jiew, who seemed to be inside the house. He had to shout several times before a response came from the room next to mine. The voice was groggy, as if the person had just woken up. I went in my room and shut the door. Out in the main area, the man continued sternly, "Wake up already, Jiew. A guest has just arrived." There was a single "yeah" in reply from the adjoining room and then silence. The nagging from beyond the door didn't relent: "Come take care of the kitchen and bathroom. Dishes are piled up everywhere, and the hot water hasn't been boiled."

I went through my bag and laid out my clothes. The voice outside my room was still barking orders to do this, that, and the other. It grated on my nerves, and my mood soured the longer I was forced to hear it. How rude! As a guest, I didn't simply want a room but a relaxing environment. I bristled—how irritating that I'd ended up in a house with a couple that liked to argue. As that thought was going through my mind, yet another voice joined the fray, a little girl shouting outside the front door.

"Pa, Pa, Pa, I came for my money."

The owner then started to haggle with the girl.

I quickly changed into a pair of shorts and a tank top. As I was leaving my room, the door next to mine opened. Naturally, I glanced in that direction: a woman was emerging from the room, her hair in such a mess that it obscured her face. She was wearing one of those old-fashioned *kawgrachow* tops in blue and a green-and-yellow floral sarong, which she proceeded to undo and rewrap while I had my back turned to lock my door. In the process, she folded it over the bottom of her blouse so that it was snug to her body. Her clothes thus adjusted, she headed toward the kitchen. I couldn't take my eyes off her. I can't say anything about her face, but her waist, buttocks, and hips, over which the flimsy sarong was pulled tight, were ample in all the right places. I needed all my strength to tear my eyes away, and even then, I looked back again after a breath. I caught another glimpse of her as she walked through the kitchen doorway and disappeared. That last glimpse was crucial because it gave me a side view of her in motion. Her sleeveless blouse, which should normally balloon out, had been tucked in tight, and the bouncing of her chest revealed that the top was doing double duty as a blouse and a bra.

I walked out the front door, went down the steps, and passed, somewhat in a daze, the father and daughter, still bickering over money. First thing on my list was a relaxing massage: I had been planning to look for a young and, most importantly, attractive masseuse to help improve my spirits. But now, suddenly, this no longer interested me. I'd become bewitched by that *kawgrachow* top and floral sarong. It was like I'd come across a statue that had hypnotized me . . . Had I lost my mind? She was just a woman from the village. I started to wonder at myself. Earlier, when I'd been walking along the beach teeming with tourists, there were Thai and *farang* women as far as the eye could see, flaunting their bodies in tiny bathing suits, and I'd looked on with only mild amusement. How was it that a common local woman, albeit one with an incredible body, had been the one to catch my eye? I somehow managed to find my way back to the beach despite being absorbed in my thoughts and not paying any attention to where I was going. There were several Western women sunbathing topless, wearing only their minuscule bikini bottoms and sunglasses. I stole several glances at them to see if I'd react the same way as I had with the local woman. I kept strolling along and browsing, but to no effect. It was as if I'd become indifferent to such things. Well, that wasn't it, because even though I was a long way from the guesthouse, my mind kept wandering off, hell-bent on circling back there. When I thought about it, I had to laugh at myself for becoming so obsessed. I hadn't even seen the woman's face, but I supposed I'd been so taken with her because of her stunning figure, which was to my exact taste . . . I sighed, shaking my head at these wild thoughts, which were inevitably useless. The woman from the village already had a husband and a child. I shouldn't stir up trouble during my vacation, especially considering how little time I had.

None of the masseuses were available when I arrived. When asked, each of them told me when she'd be free. I could wait, no problem. I decided that I'd choose the one I found most attractive. I'd have to wait at least an hour, so I killed time by going to rent a beach chair. That way I could recline under the shadow of the tent until it was my turn.

I got myself a bottle of beer and a bag of snacks. I could

hear the masseuses chatting with one another in the twangy accents typical of country girls. In a way, it was cute to hear them speak, especially with their orange-and-white uniforms. These outfits were made of jersey and, for ease of movement, fit close to the body, not too baggy or skintight. I got the feeling that whoever owned this massage tent was probably pretty strict, as the uniforms were obviously designed with modesty in mind. They didn't go very well with the beachside atmosphere. The stand-up collars and high necklines quashed any hopes of glimpsing a little flesh. But I was encouraged by their pants. Although full-length, they were stretchy, allowing the women's figures to reveal themselves freely.

But the picture before my eyes caused me to feel two distinct things. I was sometimes aroused but at other times repulsed. I gathered for myself that to trigger sexual excitement, it wasn't enough for a body to be revealed; that body had to be beautiful. An unattractive body, even on conspicuous display, would only leave you with a sense of its ugliness. I sighed, and my mind flitted back to the woman in the *kawgrachow* top without my being able to do a thing about it.

Something occurred to me then: today was the first time I'd seen a younger woman wearing a sarong and a *kawgrachow* top. It took me by surprise because, in my mind, this was how aunts and grandmothers dressed. Fat aunties, scrawny grandmas with their sagging, wrinkling skin, it didn't matter: they all looked the same in their sarongs and *kawgrachow* tops. Those loose blouses, and dangling, drooping breasts, were for grandchildren, great-grandchildren even, to snuggle up against.

That was what I was used to seeing. So I'd never considered how a sexy young woman might look in such a getup.

I sat back, sipping my beer with a smile, thinking I'd figured out why I found that young woman from the village so enticing. It must have been because of her sarong and *kawgrachow* top, which accentuated her already beautiful physique even more. Her mother and grandmother might have taught her to dress that way, wearing no bra underneath and wrapping her sarong so simply, but what about tucking in the blouse? Being able to see the contour of the waist was important. To assess the beauty of a woman's hips and buttocks, you also had to look at the waist. That kind of top would normally be loose, baggy, but tucked in, it hugged her form, clearly revealing the size of her breasts. My god! I desperately wanted to get up and go back to the guesthouse. But better not. Why even bother? The most I could hope for was staring after someone else's wife. And if I stayed in her presence too long, I'd probably lose control of myself. It was best to just let it go. Tonight, I would go hunting for a girl within my price range. It shouldn't be too difficult. And then, I could beg her to put on a sarong and a *kawgrachow* top for me. That would have to suffice for the time being.

The masseuse I'd chosen seemed to be under thirty, whereas all the others looked over forty. She wasn't exactly pretty, but her youth and her fine, fair skin somewhat compensated for it. Before starting, she asked if I was sore or tense in any particular area. I told her my legs could use some work because I'd walked such a long way, and I wanted her to focus on them and my feet. She smiled in response and followed my instructions. But not long into the session, I realized that I'd made a poor choice. She massaged like a weakling, so frail and delicate. I hardly felt a thing. All the massage managed to do was scratch a little at the nagging tension.

To distract myself, I tried to make conversation. She was nervous and shy at everything I asked, giggling bashfully before she answered each time. Significantly, her hands would stop working whenever she was replying to a question, and they would start up again only when she'd finished responding. It seemed to me like she was trying to put off work. I didn't complain because I didn't exactly pick her based on what I thought her massaging skills would be. But her laugh, it just wasn't pleasant, and she always felt the need to laugh before saying anything. In the end, I chose to remain silent because I couldn't stand that laugh. She was obviously a timid, naive girl who knew nothing about the art of seduction.

Annoyed, I decided to close my eyes, letting her continue the massage just to pass the time. In my hopeless fantasy, I was secretly thinking that if my masseuse were that woman from the village, this right here would have been heaven. Even just imagining it, I was beaming.

I was finished with the massage at four p.m. and went for a swim in the ocean for about fifteen minutes before heading back to the guesthouse. On the way back, I started to come up with a plan for the next day. I thought of a woman I'd met last year who worked at a bar on a little beach. We'd had a nice time together. Tomorrow, I would go across to the mainland and pay her a visit. The beach over there wasn't particularly beautiful, but it was bound to be more peaceful than here. I still had two days left. It'd be better than sticking it out here, wasting my time.

I stopped walking, stopped thinking, because I turned and saw something: a blue *kawgrachow* top, a green-and-yellow floral sarong, and long flowing hair. She was shaking out a large blanket to lay on the sand. I watched as she secured it from the wind by placing rocks on all four corners. A young Western woman in a dark blue bikini went to lie facedown on the blanket. My village woman carried a basket over and set it down nearby. Then she kneeled down next to the *ma'am* and unhooked her top . . . Was she actually a masseuse? I gasped, full of regret. Why didn't she say she was a masseuse? I'd unwittingly paid for my stupidity. How infuriating. But there was time, if I decided to stay a day longer.

I couldn't just walk away, so I found a spot to sit down. This time I was bent on getting my eyes' fill of her. Earlier, as I recalled, her husband had called her Jiew.

Jiew handed a small pillow to the *ma'am* for her to rest her head on. Then she gathered her own hair and tied it back. The way she sat on her heels with both arms raised accentuated every curve on her body. What I'd caught a glimpse of that afternoon wasn't just in my head, and now I was getting a good look at her face. She was beautiful . . . not in a sweet way like Thais, not in a sharp-featured way like Middle Easterners, and not in a cute way like most Asians. How odd—I thought she looked like an indigenous islander of some kind. Her skin was smooth and brown; her eyes long and tapering; her nose had a defined bridge, with the tip a touch upturned; and her lips weren't big but had a distinct shape. When she had her arms up, I noticed the muscles there and in her shoulders: this was no delicate flower of a girl but a woman, full-bodied and robust. Her hips and shoulders had a broad elegance about them; her waist was small, her stomach perfectly flat. Would other people see what I saw? That this woman was exceedingly beautiful and alluring? Who else would notice that the top and sarong she was wearing only appeared to be demure but were in fact immensely revealing? They were just thin veils of fabric on her body, with no weight holding them in place—look at them. I had eyes only for the masseuse and didn't even glance at the *farang* girl lying prone in her bikini, practically naked now with her top undone. But that sort of baring of the flesh, at a beach tourist destination like this, was so commonplace that you grew immune to it. It simply failed to arouse.

Jiew rubbed oil over the entire plane of the woman's back and slowly kneaded, putting weight on her arms and hands at measured intervals. My eyes were on her backside and hips, which moved up and down constantly. From time to time, I had to force myself to look away, for fear that I would be overcome by the desire to run over and take her in my arms. One of those times when I had to avert my eyes, I saw something else that startled me. Not far away, the short man who owned the guesthouse was in the middle of massaging the base of a long-haired male westerner's neck. Was he a masseuse, too? As it turned out, this husband and wife pair were both masseuses. The husband was working on a man and the wife a woman. Was this by design or a coincidence? If it were the former, would my secret wish to have Jiew massage me even be possible? Maybe her husband wouldn't allow it, and he might give me the massage himself. If I were to specify that I wanted a massage from her, would that be unseemly? Look at that—I was fuming at the sight—such a stunning woman with a short, dark guy who looked like the controlling type to me. If I knew her any better, I'd ask her to run away with me. Since her husband was so close, I had to be more discreet. Staring at Jiew meant having to stare at him, too. At one point, I caught her giving him a sidelong glance and even a little smile. When I looked over at her husband, my heart dropped. He was busy stretching the *farang*'s arms and shoulders and didn't even look up. Rather, it was that long-haired westerner who was smiling and ogling at her. That idiot was asking for trouble. Her husband was in the middle of giving him a massage, and he still gawked at the wife. I observed the situation, my mind churning. Jiew was really something else. The woman was bold—she'd dared to make eyes at somebody else right in front of her husband. If that was how things were, I had some hope left.

After working on the woman's back, Jiew scooted down to her legs. She spread them, sat in between, and used both hands to press down on the hips, slowly working her way down to the calves and Achilles tendons. Once she was finished, she tapped her customer to flip over. Jiew then got on her knees and lifted the woman's left leg up, placing the heel on her shoulder and hugging the leg tight. This move really got my attention. My masseuse hadn't done anything like that to me. I noticed that Jiew held the leg so it wouldn't bend at the knee and then leaned into it with her shoulder to make the leg more vertical to the ground. Oh, how tightly she squeezed that leg to her chest! Tomorrow, I absolutely had to find a way to get a massage from her.

The male *farang*'s massage finished first. As he was walking away, he felt the need to peek back at Jiew one more time. The husband shook out his blanket, collected his supplies, and put them together with the items in her basket. He stretched and then plunked himself down near her, his legs comfortably out in front of him as he casually looked around. I turned away, thinking I should probably head back and shower. Once the massage was over, both of them would surely return to look after guests like me.

The door to the guesthouse was open, the television blaring from inside. I rinsed my feet and went up into the house, where I saw a young *farang* couple watching an action movie, cans of beer in their hands. They turned and gave me a little smile. I could hear someone moving around in the kitchen. As it turned out, the cook was a middle-aged woman, not Jiew as I'd thought.

By the time I'd showered, the owners still hadn't come back. I sat on the porch waiting for them, wanting to ask about renting the room for another two nights. The sky was beginning to get dark. On the little street in front of the house, people were walking around, a mix of locals and tourists, I noticed. I was beginning to get the picture: the entire village, it seemed, was adjusting to meet the demand from tourists spilling over from the beachfront. The locals were renting out individual rooms to them—mom-and-pop operations, like a cross between guesthouses and homestays. These places didn't have signage, and they hadn't made improvements to accommodate tourists. The grocery down the way was particularly bustling. On a bench out front, three westerners were sitting in a row, tipping their beer bottles back from time to time.

The short man was back. I was crestfallen to see he'd returned by himself. I wasted no time asking him about the possibility of extending my stay, but it was too late. The two nights had been snapped up by somebody else. If I wanted to stay, it would have to be the subsequent nights. I could only shake my head because I didn't have that much time. What a shame that I'd made the wrong decision. Once again, I was paying for my stupidity. All I could do was accept the news with my head bowed and retreat to come up with a new plan. I was in a truly terrible mood by this point, but I tried to stay positive to not ruin my vacation entirely. I reminded myself that I'd made up my mind to go back to the mainland tomorrow and visit that woman, but I'd gotten sidetracked and started thinking nonsense when I saw Jiew again. I shouldn't get too worked up because ultimately all I'd get was to have her massage me for an hour or two—that was it.

I needed to let it go, to stay my course—that would be best. To prevent myself from changing my mind yet again, I called the girl I intended to visit, to gauge from her voice whether she was up for meeting me tomorrow. She accepted immediately and enthusiastically, repeating that she'd been thinking about it for ages. I chuckled, and felt my confidence revive little by little. We teased and flirted, rekindling the past, neither of us keen to hang up. I got up and walked over to the grocery, bought three cans of beer, and came back to the porch. I sat there drinking and chatting on the phone for another half hour before we said goodnight.

Feeling better, I got ready to go and do some evening scouting of the beach. I would have been on my way had I not passed right by the owner, who was standing there talking on his cell phone. He said to Jiew that she should hurry back straight away because there was a client who wanted to take the whole night. I stopped in my tracks. When I looked up, I saw that young, long-haired *farang* hanging around awkwardly in front of the house. I stood still, processing the whole scene. I'd definitely heard it right. He told Jiew to hurry back because someone had asked to take the whole night. I wanted to keep walking, but my body wouldn't budge. It was as if a part of my mind were commanding me to turn around, walk back up to the house, and slump down in one corner of the porch to keep watch.

I had to see it with my own eyes: What was the actual situation? What had I misunderstood? Was Jiew *not* the owner's wife? I could hardly believe she was a woman who sold her services. I kept my eyes on the *farang*. He was standing there waiting patiently, his right hand holding a cigarette and his left hand in his pants pocket. Casually on his feet, he had his face slightly upturned, trying to come off cool to passersby. I wanted to vomit just looking at him.

Here she came. She was walking empty-handed, the basket with her massage supplies nowhere to be seen. Her arrival prompted a smile from the *farang*, who made no move toward her. Jiew was the one to approach him, grace him with a smile, and say a few words. He nodded and stepped closer, planting a kiss on her left cheek. Eyes shining, she smiled and led him inside the house by the hand. She then signaled him to sit down and wait on the porch while she went into the room next to mine. A moment later, she reemerged in a sarong and with a towel thrown over her shoulders and walked through the kitchen to the bathroom. While I was observing, the *farang* was watching, too. He sprang up to follow her. But me, I wasn't allowed. All I could do was sink back in my seat like a fool. What could I do but berate myself? I'm an idiot, a stupid, stupid idiot. It served me right. I might as well forget about having any of my dreams come true. By now that damn *farang* was probably having the time of his life helping Jiew shower. I got up in a huff and stormed over to the grocery and bought a six-pack. I took the beers back to the porch and started drinking. Why was I so stupid?

I went into the kitchen, pretending to look for something, but in truth I wanted to spy on what was happening in the bathroom area. As it happened, Jiew wasn't showering in the bathroom. She was using the shower on the cement landing, and the *farang* guy was sitting on the steps leading down from the kitchen, smoking. I could hear her chatting with him in halting English, and I could hear him laughing, enjoying himself. I went back to the porch. There was nothing I could do but throw back another beer. A while later, Jiew led the man into the room and shut the door.

I must have gone insane. Instead of going out for a stroll, to enjoy food and drink and the lively beachside ambience, I went and locked myself in my room. I put my ear against the wall, trying to eavesdrop on them. When I ran out of beer, I went to buy more. I drank until I passed out. What a depressing vacation.

A KNOCK ON the door woke me up. When I grabbed my watch and looked at it, I realized it was already eleven a.m. I quickly jumped out of bed and stuffed my things into my bag. Once I opened the door, I saw the situation: two Asian girls, I'm not sure from what country, were waiting for my room, and Jiew, now in a dark blue *kaw-grachow* top and a red-and-black sarong, was standing there like a housekeeper waiting to clean. With fresh sheets slung over her left arm, she smiled and told me to take my time—just remove my bag and from there I could use the bathroom and have some coffee at my leisure. I nodded to show I'd heard but didn't look her in the eye. Jiew walked past me to go clean the room. Me, I went to the bathroom to get ready. Right now my objective was clearer than anything: get to the mainland fast and go meet the woman I'd made plans with.

All set to leave, I swung my backpack on and got going right away. The short man was at the door to see me off. "Thank you, sir. Best of luck." I forced a smile. If only! Staying here, I couldn't catch a break. Down the street, there was a local stir-fry and curry joint. I stopped in to have a bite since it was on the way, and I didn't want to lose any time going to one of the fancy places on the beach. I felt a breeze from the west as I was eating, a huge relief from the heat. Fifteen minutes later, as I was paying for the food, a woman walked by. I didn't know if my eyes were playing tricks on me, but I swore it was Jiew. From the way she was dressed, though, it seemed unlikely. I stood up and headed out. I was so head-down-focused on walking that it took me a while to realize that I was following the woman from a moment ago. From behind, I saw a loose braid under a white baseball cap, a white button-down with the sleeves casually rolled up, navy-blue cargo pants, and sturdy closed-backed shoes in blue and white. My stride was longer and quicker than hers so I was gradually catching up. Part of me thought it was Jiew, but another part of me thought it couldn't be—I'd just seen her in a sarong a little while ago. And even if it was, so be it. I wasn't going to lose my head again. I sped up, trying to overtake her. She glanced back when she realized someone was on her heels.

It really was Jiew. She smiled upon recognizing me. I smiled back, just enough to be polite. She asked me why I was rushing back. I'd almost passed her but because she struck up a conversation, we ended up walking side by side. Now the sun suddenly disappeared, even though it had been beating down a minute ago. We both looked up, seeing dark clouds spreading over half the sky. With stiff winds, the clouds were moving quickly. I couldn't believe it was going to rain.

"I only reserved the room for one night. I was thinking about extending, but I decided too late," I told her.

"Really? Do you want to stay on? I could probably find something for you," Jiew said, her expression earnest.

"It's okay. I've already made other plans. What about you? Are you on your way to do massages by the beach?"

"I'm off today. I have to go give my mother a massage in the hospital."

"Oh, really? Is she all right?"

"She had a stroke. She can't move the left side of her body."

I nodded. I didn't know what else to say. We walked on together in silence, heading for the pier. The woman

I'd been infatuated with yesterday, today she was walking right next to me. She had such an open, honest way of speaking that you'd never be able to tell that she was a prostitute. When I really thought about it, she was one hardworking woman. She took care of the guesthouse in the morning, and in the afternoon she worked as a masseuse. When night fell, she sold her services. And on top of that, she had to look after her mother who was sick in the hospital . . . Learning these things made me more aware of the other aspects of her person. The only catch was, us men, if all we wanted was to sleep with a woman, we should avoid learning too many details about her, or our lust would dissolve into other feelings.

We quickened our pace because of the rain. From the wind, it seemed a storm was upon us. By the time we reached the pier, we were soaked. No ferry would be coming in or out until the weather cleared. Even under the roof, everything was being sprayed by the rain, now blowing sideways. The sea appeared misty and white, and you couldn't see very far out. We went over to a bench that seemed a good spot to escape the downpour. As soon as we sat down, Jiew struck up a conversation again.

"If you really aren't in a hurry to leave and you don't mind not having a private room, we could arrange a sleeping area in the main part of the house and even put up a mosquito net for you. You could also rent a tent and sleep on the beach," she suggested.

I started to waver. "But don't you need to look after your mother? How would you be able to arrange it for me?"

She laughed. "I'd just call the guesthouse and let them know. Then it'd be all set."

I listened, not yet responding to her offer. Between the moment we'd started walking together and now, sitting here getting misted by the rain, I'd been discreetly studying her. Today she seemed like a friendly, sincere average local woman. It was curious how her sexuality, so palpable yesterday, had completely vanished. Perhaps it was due to her clothing, or perhaps she fully intended the effect—when she wasn't working, she didn't need to turn on her charms. Or perhaps it was me: so angered and embarrassed by my own stupidity that I'd lost my desire. I couldn't deny that there may have been a more perverse reason for my waning interest: my discovery that Jiew was a prostitute, not the wife of a local as I'd initially understood. The thought made me flinch. How could I be so vile? I'd been completely consumed by lust, by my desire to sleep with someone else's wife. But once I realized her trade, and the fact that I could actually have her, I'd lost all interest, just like that.

I never responded about extending my stay; we just chatted about the weather. It rained for an incredibly long time. A handful of locals were the only other people waiting for the ferry. Because it was Saturday, I seemed to be the only tourist who wanted to leave. Jiew went back and forth between talking with me and occasionally greeting other people, mostly ferrymen and longshoremen. There were some playful exchanges but nothing indecent. Other than that, they talked casually, like people from the same hometown who were well acquainted with one another.

I observed her the entire time. One thing puzzled me.

I didn't know how Jiew managed it—how was it possible that none of these men, who must surely be aware of her profession, ever verbally crossed the line or behaved inappropriately toward her, even a little? I'd come across plenty of prostitutes, and I'd seen enough of how men treated them, so I found it hard to believe that on a day when such a woman was off duty, every man would just stop viewing her in those terms. Was our conscience really so evolved?

I finally boarded the ferry at three in the afternoon. I again sat beside Jiew, but this time I did it on purpose. I wanted to act more forward. Since I thought of her as a friend now, I wanted to tell her how I'd been feeling before.

"Did you notice me at all yesterday?" I asked her bluntly.

"Of course. I saw you throughout the day," she replied, not yet understanding what I was getting at.

"I don't know what came over me. I'd never seen a young woman in a sarong and a *kawgrachow* top before. Seeing you in that outfit . . . I was completely beside myself."

She laughed. "No wonder! I saw you sitting there watching me while I was giving a massage."

"Yes. I'll be honest. Yesterday, I really wanted to sleep with you because of that outfit you were wearing."

"Really? Just because of my outfit?" she said with a laugh as she looked at me fondly.

"I'm serious. When you were dressed that way, you— forgive me—you looked incredibly sexy. Yesterday while I was getting a massage on the beach, I closed my eyes and imagined that the masseuse was you."

"Oh, you got a massage yesterday? You should have told me."

I sighed. "I didn't know! It was so infuriating. I only realized when I was walking back and saw you massaging that Western woman. I watched you for ages. That was when I decided to extend my stay, just so I could get a massage with you."

"If you want to get a massage with me, why don't you stay?"

"But tonight you have to go take care of your mother."

"I'll be back tomorrow morning."

"How much would it cost?"

"There's three hundred, five hundred, or seven hundred, up to you."

"And if I wanted to hire you for the whole night?"

She shook her head, smiling. "That's not possible."

I was taken aback but decided to ask again to be sure. "No? How come?"

"It'd just be a massage. Nothing overnight."

I was confused. I looked at her, and she stared back, completely serious. "But last night you spent the night with that *farang*."

"Yes, foreign tourists only. I don't take other Thais."

I didn't understand, but chose not to react, keeping silent because her comment had sickened me to the point of outrage. I looked out on the water, eager to reach the shore. I could tell that Jiew was troubled by my reaction, which only stoked my anger. Did it make her feel superior pitting Thai and foreign men against each other like this? At the end of the day, a whore was a whore. As we approached the pier, I grabbed my bag, readying myself to be the first passenger off the boat without saying goodbye.

From there, I went to catch the *songthaew* jitney to go to a town nearby. Jiew followed behind, heading to the jitney station as well. Just my luck. Could I not escape her? Because I was still so furious, I marched over to her. "What do you have against sleeping with Thai people?" I asked bitterly.

She sighed and looked around, as if concerned about discussing this topic by the side of the road. But because of my serious tone, she answered me.

"I don't sleep with Thai men because the island's a small world. Pretty much everyone knows one another. If I accepted Thai clients, it'd be difficult to turn down the locals. The *farangs*, they come and go in no time. But with Thai people or people from the island, we have to live together, have to see each other's face until we're old and gray. The fact that I'm a prostitute to westerners . . . it's something temporary. We meet, then we go our separate ways. But if you're a prostitute in your hometown, that's what you'll be until the day you die. Even if you quit, people will still look at you the same way. People who have slept with you and who still run into you every day, how are they going to forget? I just want to make enough money, and then I'll quit. I'm still hoping that I'll have a nice family, have children. Maybe there'll be a good man on the island who can accept me. Then he can be with me without having to worry if I'd slept with his friends or his family members before."

She waited for my reaction. Seeing that I was stunned and at a loss for words, she said that she had to get to the hospital and then ran over to the jitney. The driver honked, asking me if I was going to board. I just stared at him blankly, my mouth hanging open, feeling as heavy as a stone pestle. The *songthaew* pulled out and left.

EARLY THE NEXT day, I was sitting on the porch of the guesthouse, tapping my foot. Jiew came back at eight in the morning. She was surprised to see me. I smiled sheepishly and was quick to tell her how sorry I was. She said no apology was necessary—that she wasn't upset, that this sort of thing happened so often she'd grown used to it.

"In that case, can I get a massage with you?"

She smiled immediately, a different smile from the one I'd seen her give the *farang* the other day.

"Right now?"

"Whenever. It's fine if you need to take care of other stuff first."

"I'll just be a moment." She quickly went off. I watched her go, eyeing her every move.

Today was Sunday. The Western couple and the pair of Asian girls had all gone to the beach. A middle-aged lady was carrying a grocery basket into the kitchen. Children, both boys and girls, were waiting to settle their accounts with the owner of the guesthouse. These were children who hawked knickknacks on the beach, relying on the investment of the proprietor, whom they called Pa. As Pa opened his ledger, the kids swarmed him, forming a tight cluster near the steps.

Jiew had been gone for a while. When she reappeared, she was wearing a lavender *kawgrachow* top and a sarong the color of a jewel beetle. Her hair, long and still wet, was messy from having been rubbed with a towel. A lovely scent of soap and shampoo emanated from her whole body. The old Jiew, achingly seductive, was back, revived by her traditional attire. She asked me if I wanted my massage here or by the beach. I chose here, concerned that if we went to the waterfront, a *farang* might come and distract her. Jiew left for a moment and returned with her basket of massage supplies. She laid a straw mat down in the common area and put a blanket over it. After having me change out of my pants and into shorts, she asked if I wanted an oil massage or a standard one. I chose the standard, for fear that the oil would mask the scent of her body.

I lay on my back, with Jiew sitting behind my head. Her cool hands began massaging my forehead and eyebrows. I let my mind and body relax. She pressed lightly, going from my forehead to the top of my eyebrows and out around my eyes, and then moving over to my temples and scalp. She tucked her hands under to massage the base of my neck, working her way down to my shoulders.

To make conversation, she asked where I'd stayed the night before.

"I slept on the beach. I stayed up late drinking so I rented a chair and fell asleep. I walked over here in the morning to take a shower and have some coffee."

She started massaging my left arm, shoulder, wrist, and hand. She committed to the massage—this was a strong woman, and she wasn't holding back. Before long, the squeezes, presses, and pulls of her hands created an unintended effect: instead of relaxing, I became increasingly tense. Her pleasant smell and her touch sent me into a state of nervous arousal. I tried to control myself. Each time she removed her hands, it was as if an alarm went off in my head, reminding me to pull it together. Oh god, I was going to have to brace myself for a tougher fight if I was going to keep my body under control.

Jiew stationed herself at the tips of my feet. I felt more relaxed with her a bit farther away. Once I calmed myself down, I realized how steady the pressure from her hands had been this entire time. She was young but her skills as a masseuse were top-notch. She moved up to my calves and knees: squeeze, squeeze, squeeze, and then press, squeeze, squeeze, squeeze, and then press, running her hands up and down several times. Not again! My manhood began to pester me again. But how could I blame it? My desire had been building so fiercely inside of me all weekend, and kept so bottled up, how could it not burst out at the first opportunity? I started to worry . . . I doubted I could keep it in check for long. And she was only working on my feet and legs.

Jiew bent my left knee so it was pointing toward the ceiling, and started to massage down from the calf to the Achilles tendon. A while later, she switched to the right leg. But how would she massage my thighs? Would she sit in between my legs like I'd seen her do with that Western lady? Thankfully no: she merely sat to the side and squeezed my thighs one at a time. Then it occurred to me that when the *ma'am* had her legs spread, she had actually been lying facedown. I suffered through the massage, feeling Jiew's hands dangerously close to my groin, and something down there was beginning to stir. I fought hard to control it, but my efforts were in vain. After a while, I began counting. I told myself that if I got to five and Jiew still hadn't moved on, I'd excuse myself and go to the bathroom. Luckily, she suddenly changed maneuvers. I opened my eyes, letting my body unclench. Saved at the very last second. When I glanced at her, I noticed a slight smile, and I was mortified. Had she seen? She caught me looking at her, and flashed me a smile before continuing the massage. Now she configured my legs into a number four shape, with the left leg folded over the right, and leaned her weight onto the ball of my left foot. A moment later, it was the other side's turn. She continued stretching my legs in different ways for several minutes, perhaps giving me time to compose myself.

Finally, we got to the position I was most interested in. She lifted my right leg and rested the heel on her shoulder. With her arms wrapped around the leg, she slowly leaned forward, making it increasingly perpendicular to the ground. I watched her; she was singularly focused on the massage, nothing more. I was gripped with a sudden sense of shame as it occurred to me: Was this how she massaged her mother in the hospital? Was this how patients with paralysis were massaged? Jiew set my right leg down and moved to the left. I waved my hand in protest, saying, "That will do. I really should be going."

She told me the price, five hundred baht, and asked how the massage was and if I felt any more relaxed.

I chuckled as I got my money out, not knowing how to respond. But when I saw that she was earnestly waiting for an answer, I gave her an honest compliment: the massage was excellent.

Jiew beamed when I handed her seven hundred baht.

We nodded, bidding each other farewell. I carried my bag to the stairs and sat down to put on my sneakers. With the cash in hand, she walked over to the porch, where the owner of the guesthouse was still absorbed in his ledger. She stuck out her palm, asking for the remainder of what she was owed.

"I'm so lucky. I settled the hospital bill yesterday, and I still have a whole five hundred baht left. Plus I got another seven hundred for the massage. What a relief! And there are no more bills to pay today." She tapped the money on her cheek and then leaned over the railing to say to me, "Thanks again for coming back for the massage."

I smiled at her. "Yes, my pleasure." I looked at her one last time before walking away. My final image of Jiew, her face over the porch railing, was nothing like the seductive young woman I'd first met, but merely a hardworking person who had a tough life. I realized that, with women you'll never stand a chance of sleeping with, it's better to learn as much as you can about them, until lust gives way to other feelings.

WOOD CHILDREN

PRAKORB WOKE UP SUDDENLY DURING THE NIGHT. HE didn't feel for anyone next to him because a dim light was still on in the room. From behind where Mala was sitting, he saw her shadow in a corner, pitch-black and sharp since she was blocking the lamp. The glowing light formed a halo around her, as though she were cradling a luminous glass ball in her hands. Mala was hunched over, her head bowed low, her arms and shoulders constantly moving. The round stool she was sitting on was ill-proportioned to the table.

Prakorb reached for the alarm clock. He nearly gasped: it was almost three in the morning. Troubled, he sighed, turning his back to the scene in the corner and closing his eyes, even though he no longer felt sleepy. He knew how much Mala wanted to have a child. She'd expressed it often the first year they were married. But after trying for one year, Mala had begun to realize that conceiving wasn't going to be easy. She talked to him less about it. Now Mala had lived with him for a full six years, and they still didn't have any children. She never brought up the topic anymore. Prakorb worked so hard that he rarely ever had a day off. As for Mala, she stayed at home and performed her duties as a housewife impeccably. He had never once seen any nook or cranny of the house looking less than tidy. Mala also loved gardening. Prakorb was happy that she had found something to occupy herself with. He didn't want his wife to wallow in the sadness brought on by her longing for a child, which he knew she still concealed in her heart.

But Mala had changed. She wasn't dedicating herself to housework and gardening like before. One day Prakorb had come home to find a new table in the corner of their spacious bedroom, which already contained his desk. Piled on top, there were cylindrical pieces of wood six or seven inches in length and three or four inches in diameter; a short, sharp knife with a pointed end and a large handle easy to grip, the blade itself two inches long; plus several chisels. Mala had told him wood carving was something she'd dreamed of doing for a long time, and now she felt more compelled than ever to go ahead and do it. He remembered being completely caught off guard that day. He had never known that Mala enjoyed it.

"What are you working on?" Prakorb had asked. "I don't see a model there." But Mala hadn't answered; she had merely smiled without looking him in the face.

A week later, Prakorb had gotten to see Mala's first piece of work, which was downright awful. Not only was it crooked, its proportions were off, and the details didn't look realistic. But despite the poor quality of her work, he could tell immediately that Mala had intended to carve a child. He had stared at the carving for a long time, deeply pained. Mala had obviously poured a great deal of effort into it; perhaps it had come from pent-up energy over the last six years. He realized that Mala had probably wasted ten or twenty pieces of wood before she had produced her first passable carving. He hadn't understood what she'd been thinking: Once it was clear that she had miscarved, why had she insisted on finishing it? Or maybe her goal wasn't for the piece to be perfect?

Over the past several months, Mala had carved almost ten figures. Children formed out of wood, in different poses, were lined up on her table. Some of them smiled, lopsided mouths and all; some had heads that skewed back, hands that didn't align with the arms, or feet that were disproportionately large. Mala was pleased with all these figures, spending most of her days stooped over on that round stool, never appearing to get sore. She did chores around the house in a frantic manner, but sometimes paused midtask, her eyes off somewhere else. When she caught herself, she quickly got back to work so she could return to the wood children she was making as soon as possible.

Prakorb knew he had to do something to improve the situation between them. He brooded, his mind aglow beneath his closed eyelids. He tried to figure out why Mala never discussed having children with him anymore. She kept that consuming desire all to herself. This behavior led him to believe that it was perhaps his fault, and that was why she was upset and acting antagonistically toward him. Prakorb tried to shake the thought: it was rather this line of thinking that was antagonistic toward her. He sighed, feeling helpless as he lay worn out in bed, his breathing shallow. Every time he agonized over their relationship, unable to say or do a thing, he felt like a feeble old man. Prakorb's eyes widened—perhaps he was too old. He had often considered his age, but it had never alarmed him as much as it did this time. He had turned fifty this year, but Mala was only thirty-one. She was still young, her body able; she even looked younger than her years. Little by little, he was gaining clarity. She blamed him, didn't she? She thought he was the reason they couldn't have children, and that was why she refused to broach the subject. It was because he was too old, wasn't it?

Prakorb sensed Mala get into bed when it was almost dawn. Within two minutes, she was sound asleep; he could hear her breathing evenly. A short while later, he got up to shower. Out of habit, he always rose early. He'd decided to take the day off because he wanted to stay home and spend time with Mala. They might not have children, but their married life couldn't languish as a result. He loved Mala, and there was no way he was going to let her distance herself any more than she already had.

MALA WOKE UP shortly before noon. She didn't see Prakorb and assumed he had gone to work as usual. The house felt so empty and hushed, and her loneliness was unbearable. Something was amiss in her marriage: she was simply living out the days, waiting for time to pass, as old age gradually crept closer. She had only been married six years, yet in that amount of time, she already felt alone. What was more, the age difference between her and Prakorb was distressing: When his time eventually came and he left her behind, how was she supposed to go on—especially when they didn't have children?

Once she had taken care of all the household chores, Mala went back to her carving table as usual. She had just completed her tenth wood child last night. This one had an expressionless face, neither smiling nor crying, and stood with its head cocked, as if curious. Mala was happy with the result. She thought that children who appeared impassive were more intriguing; they gave her the impression that they concealed their feelings from the world. These were the children who were full of imagination and whose minds searched far and wide for things to ponder, yet no one could discern their thoughts. Mala smiled. She picked up a new piece of wood and stood it on its end as she tried to conjure up images of children. Then a picture came to her of a giggling newborn, squirming in a cradle with its hands punching and its feet kicking the air. She laid the wood down on its side, trying to visualize the baby trapped within. Mala grabbed her knife and used the sharp point to slice into the wood. After forming the general shape, she began to chisel away the unwanted bits.

Mala's hand froze when she heard Prakorb calling her name. She hollered in reply, her curiosity piqued. He wanted her to come down. But why wasn't he coming into the bedroom? What had he forgotten? She left the room and walked around the entire house looking for him, but he was nowhere to be found. Then she heard him again, asking her to open the front door.

When she did, Mala was speechless at the sight before her. Prakorb was standing there with a smile, his left arm supporting a child against his waist, his right hand carrying several bags of takeout. The little boy stared at her with his bright round eyes, a piece of candy nestled in one cheek.

"Can you take something? My arms are about to fall off," Prakorb said. Mala hesitated, not knowing what to grab. He laughed and went to give her the child, but when Mala opened her arms, the boy wriggled free and ran into the yard.

"Whose kid is that?" Mala kept her eyes trained on the boy.

"He's the son of one of my construction workers. He's a cute kid, very clever. He takes a while to warm up to people, but once he gets comfortable with you, he's really talkative," Prakorb said. "He has a bit of a naughty side, so his mother spanks him a lot. When he's with her, he's a crybaby and whines for attention. He knows me well because we see each other often. I've already scrubbed off a layer of grime. If you'd only seen him earlier! He was so filthy you couldn't tell if he was dark- or light-skinned," Prakorb went on animatedly.

"Are you thinking of possibly adopting him?" Mala asked.

"No, no. I just think he's cute, and I thought it might be nice for you to have some company, that's all," Prakorb said. "I told his mother I'd take him home this evening. Go ahead, get to know him. He really is adorable. I'll take this stuff in and lay everything out." Then he went inside the house, leaving Mala and the boy alone.

From the window, Prakorb covertly watched them. Mala seemed overjoyed. She was bonding with the child quickly, and the two played together in the yard for ages. He could faintly hear Mala's laughter from time to time. Until today, he had never seen her laugh so hard, or look so cheerful. Ultimately Prakorb wanted Mala to be happy. This scenario seemed more realistic and closer to her dream than being cooped up with those distorted, lifeless wood children. He couldn't predict how his decision to bring the boy over might affect their relationship down the road, but he believed in that instant, seeing how happy Mala was spending time with the child, that her joy was, in part, his doing. Mala would continue to be with him, stay close to him. The misshapen wood children had caused her to pull away and cling to that table, but he was going to lure her back—back to the real world, to real happiness.

Right then Prakorb went upstairs to their bedroom. He eyed those wood children with contempt, a contempt that extended even to the knife, the chisels, the raw wood, the table, the stool—all the way to the crate that Mala kept under the table for scraps. He desperately wanted to banish these things from their lives that very moment, but he knew he had to refrain for now; he had to stay cool. All of it would be gently erased from Mala's mind, without her even realizing it. But in truth he was eager to discover the outcome: Between the wood children and the bundle of joy he had brought her, which would she find more important?

Prakorb considered each item on the table in turn. He grabbed one of the wood children but then changed his mind and quickly put it down. He felt so nervous that he had to console himself: He wasn't a child misbehaving, but an adult fixing a problem. What he was about to do, he was simply making things right, not doing anything wrong. He chose again—this time the knife. He hurried to the window and pushed it open. Their bedroom was on the second floor; beyond the fence, he could see the little canal, its surface covered with water lettuce and duckweeds. He threw the knife out the window with all his strength. As it flew through the air, something deep inside him told him no, and he was tempted to snatch it back. Prakorb quickly suppressed the feeling. In any case, it was too late. He saw the green carpet of duckweed ripple slightly, and the knife disappeared. The leaves smoothed back together, serene as though they'd never been disturbed. He closed the window and left the room, and as his nerves settled back down, he felt calm, like he hadn't done a thing.

Prakorb arranged a variety of dishes on the dining room table. It was too early for dinner, but he wanted to have the boy eat with them, and to do so early enough that he could drop him off in the evening and still return home before it got dark—before Mala would have a chance to go into the bedroom.

Mala led the boy inside the house by the hand. Her face was flushed; she was catching her breath from laughing. Gleaming beads of sweat cropped up along her hairline and dripped down the sides of her face. Prakorb was spellbound watching her. Seeing her this way made him indescribably happy. Mala said that she was going to take the boy upstairs to see the wood children.

Prakorb rushed over and picked up the boy. "Look at you, you're tired and hot," he told Mala. "Go wash up and get yourself something to drink. I'll take him to see them. I've already set the table. Let's eat a bit early today, so I can drop him off before it gets dark. You can wait for us down here. We'll be back in a minute."

Mala complied. For her, it was a day of novelty and joy—joy that only children could bring about. She was amused as her mind recalled her earlier interactions with the boy: how he had wedged himself into the farthest recesses of his mind, then looked back out at the world with a perspective that adults could never divine. When he tried to convey the images he saw, reality was bent into something curiously warped. These new perspectives fascinated her endlessly.

Dinner was something of an experiment for each participant, and everyone was happy to see it play out. They treated one another like family: the parents each tending to their little child, never taking their eyes off him. Watching them, the boy felt like he was a part of this home; he even touched and picked up everything as if he were the owner. Mala watched the boy until she felt he was really hers; Prakorb watched Mala as she took pleasure in what he had played a part in giving her.

Prakorb drove the boy home and turned right around, not wasting any time. He sped back, worried that Mala had gone up to the bedroom and realized the knife was gone. He had to admit that he felt afraid without being able to pinpoint why, and it shook him that he was so terrified.

By the time he got back, it was almost sundown. He was relieved to see Mala at the dinner table. She had cleaned up and done the dishes, and was now leaning back in one of the chairs, her arms outstretched on the table, her eyes unfocused, lost in thought. When she saw him out of the corner of her eye, a smile appeared immediately. She called him over to sit down next to her and began enthusiastically talking about the boy.

"He's such a wondrous little human being! He has these ideas that are so strange, yet fascinating. You might find them funny at first, but once you really think about them, they blow you away. For example—oh, what was it?

Oh yes, he asked me, 'Can sharks live in sugar water?'
See? Look at his question! You know why he asked that?
Because someone had told him that sharks live in *salt*
water, so he was wondering why they'd choose to live in
salt water when sugar water's tastier."

Mala laughed as she told the story. Prakorb nodded
and laughed along, making sure not to interrupt the flow.

"And another time, he asked me, 'When the sun's
down, would something bad happen if someone steps
on it?'

"I told him, 'No, the sun's very far away. People can't
walk that far.'

"Then he asked, 'What if someone walks that far and
steps on it, would something bad happen?'

"I told him, 'The sun's really big. People can't step on
it like that.'

"Then he asked, 'What about elephants? Elephants
are big. If an elephant steps on it, would something bad
happen?'

"I told him, 'It can't. The sun's big and also very hot.
If an elephant got too close, it would get hot.'

"Then he asked, 'What if the elephant doesn't get
hot? An elephant's big, too. If an elephant steps on the
sun, would the sun break?'

"I told him, 'No, the sun wouldn't break,' and you
know what he asked me next? He said, 'Why not? Is it
because the sun's squishy like a pillow so when you step
on it, it doesn't break?' Listen to him! He was so quick
I could barely keep up. His mind went to places I didn't
even know existed. But ultimately where he was going
was right here, right around us. It made me realize that if
you want to have a conversation with a child and be able

to keep up with him, you first have to learn to cast reality aside and try to view everything in a new light."

"Seeing you this happy takes a load off my mind," Prakorb told her. "I'll bring the boy over more often so you won't get lonely. Why don't you go take a shower. I'll wash your hair for you today. After that, I have something to tell you."

Curious, Mala looked at him. "Can you tell me now? What is it?"

Prakorb smiled at her. "Let's shower first. I'll shower with you, okay? I'll wash your hair. Wait for me in the bathroom. I'll go get us towels, and I'll pick out a nightgown for you, too."

Mala blushed, smiling bashfully at the implication. Her eyes full of tenderness, she watched him walk off.

Later, as they made their way from the bathroom to the bedroom, Prakorb clung to Mala like a pet protective of its owner. Before she even had a chance to put on the nightgown that he had laid out for her, he led her to the bed, keeping her in his constant embrace.

"This morning, I went to the doctor's for a checkup," Prakorb whispered into her ear. "She said everything's still working. I'm in good shape to have children, no problem. I hope you don't think I'm too old."

Mala looked at him compassionately, and she suddenly started crying out of love for him. Nuzzling up to him, she said, "Not at all, you're not old at all. I've never seen you as old. Honestly. To me, you've never been old."

MALA WOKE AT daybreak. Prakorb was already dressed and about to leave for work. He was leaving unusually early, but Mala didn't question it. As soon as she opened her eyes, her mind, now fresh, began working immediately. One image of the boy stood out: he was throwing a tantrum and being a little devil while she was trying to get him to warm up to her. His expression was impish and full of rebellion, but the more he tried to show what he was made of, the more his pureness and innocence came to the fore. This mood of his captivated her. Its contradiction seemed to blend into one harmonized whole. If she . . . if she tried to carve it, would she be able to? Would she be able to create a wood child that somehow both resisted and endeared itself to the viewer?

Mala shivered from excitement. She had already started working on an eleventh wood child, the newborn—also thrilling, and a challenge to carve. From the very beginning, she had planned to carve each piece to completion, one at a time, so that none would be left in limbo at any given point. But this case was an exception because her latest inspiration came from flesh and blood—the life and mind of a real child. She was too impassioned to hold off. She would finish the newborn, but only after she was through with the endearingly moody wood child.

Mala practically jumped out of bed. She showered and hurriedly took care of some things around the house. Within an hour, she was seated on the round stool in front of her carving table. Right away, she noticed that the knife was missing. It left her puzzled. The burst of inspiration propelling her to create that wooden sculpture couldn't be extinguished; instead it morphed into pure rage. Mala heatedly racked her brain for the cause of the knife's disappearance. The boy was her first and only suspect. She stopped thinking about the knife; after all, it could easily be replaced, and she was bound to have other rushes of inspiration. But what of that image of the boy that had taken such a concrete shape in her mind? That picture was now blurred, and she was unable to form it anew; only the boy could do that.

Convinced that the child had stolen the knife, Mala trembled with fury. That thief of a child had completely ruined her vision. His purity and innocence were gone. The wickedness within him had revealed itself and could no longer be brought back into harmony.

Mala sat still, trying to rein in her seething emotions. Perhaps she was being too rash: what was inside a little human being was often hard to comprehend. She had to be generous and leave all doors of possibilities open. If she could find a way out, the image of the boy that she thought had collapsed might still stand. Mala wanted to save it. She was going to do everything to keep it alive.

She decided to take action. She went to Prakorb's desk, took out his log book, and flipped to the most recent entries. The newest construction site was for a hotel on the main road in town; the foundation was just being laid. Mala closed the book and rushed out of the house.

Three hours later she came home. Her face bore an expression of coldness and contempt, at times that of someone suffering the pain of betrayal. She climbed into bed and lay still. After some time, she fell asleep and didn't stir until evening.

PRAKORB WAS SURPRISED to find Mala in bed. He had never seen her napping in the evening. His heart skipped a beat when he looked over at her carving table. Mala had probably realized that the knife was missing. He woke her up, wanting to see how she was doing. After yesterday, he knew in his bones that those wood children would be defeated. But when Mala awoke, she scared him with the first comment she uttered: she said that klepto kid had stolen her knife. The second frightened him even more: she said she had gone to the construction site to ask for it back, but the child had refused. Prakorb was rattled. He'd never imagined things would turn out this way. Was the knife really so important to Mala that she felt the need to go and reclaim it? He had been at the site that day, yet he hadn't heard a thing about the ordeal. She'd merely wanted that knife and had given no thought to stopping by to see him. And what about him? He'd brought the kleptomaniac child here to steal the knife from her—was that what this had turned into?

Prakorb froze in shock. When his eyes wandered to the collection of wood children, he saw some of them sneering at him, others mocking him with peculiar gestures. He gathered himself and looked away, sinking down to sit next to Mala on the bed. He had to defend the boy.

"Mala," he said, "you've got it all wrong. You shouldn't have been so hasty. The boy didn't take the knife."

Mala looked up at him immediately, her eyes confused.

"I did. I mean, I didn't take the knife on purpose. I accidentally broke it this morning so I threw it away. I forgot to tell you. I'll buy you a new one, all right?" Prakorb paused and studied his wife.

Mala's heart pounded as she replayed her actions in her mind. She had accused the child of being a thief.

Worse, she had pressured him into confessing. The boy's mother had stood there stock-still, staring at the ground, refusing to utter a single word. Mala burst into tears, detailing to Prakorb how she had wronged the child by falsely accusing him.

"All I could think was that he was refusing to own up to it. But, you know? The truth is, he's perfectly innocent! He didn't even know if he'd taken it. I pressed and pressed him until he admitted to it. But when I asked him where he'd put the knife, he just said that he didn't know, he didn't know. His mother looked so embarrassed and angry. It was unnerving how still and quiet she was the entire time. I have no idea how she's going to punish him." Mala was sobbing.

Prakorb hugged her tenderly.

"What do I do?" Mala continued, still distressed. "What should I do? I'm scared to go and tell his mother that it was all a misunderstanding. I'm scared to face her. That woman is so intimidating, one of those silent types. If she found out the truth, she'd despise me for making her punish her child. How much pain did he have to suffer for being called a thief? I'm sure he was severely punished."

"It's all right, Mala. It's all right," Prakorb consoled her. "If you're afraid, you don't have to go. It's really not a big deal. The kid's young. If he didn't even know if he took the knife or not, he's going to forget about all this in no time. As for his mother, don't worry. A mother's always going to love her child. She won't love him any less even if she thinks he's a thief. Rest easy, Mala. There's no problem here. It's just a trivial matter."

His words soothed her, and her crying tapered off.

"Children are so lucky. They switch emotions at the drop of a hat—happy, sad, mad—and they forget just as easily. Me, on the other hand, I'm going to have to live with this for the rest of my life."

"Don't worry, Mala. If you feel like you mistreated him, you can make it up to him. I'll bring him over again, and this time you have to be more loving and more caring toward him than before, you understand? You have to show your love even more, okay?"

Mala smiled at him, all trace of worry gone from her face. Prakorb tightened his embrace around her. He glanced at the wood children and smirked victoriously as he told Mala that he would bring the boy over first thing tomorrow.

PRAKORB NUDGED THE boy on the back to get him to approach Mala. Once he stood within about five feet of her, he refused to go any closer. Prakorb let Mala know that he was heading back to work and flashed her a smile on his way out. He was in high spirits; he no longer had a care in the world. Mala hadn't mentioned the knife to him again. She felt terribly guilty about the boy, and Prakorb was happy she felt that way: it meant from now on Mala would focus her attention and energy on the living instead of those ghastly wood children—and perhaps soon he and Mala would have a child of their own.

The boy still wouldn't budge. He had his chin tucked and his eyes pitched upward, staring at Mala, obviously afraid. The look in his eyes made it abundantly clear that he didn't trust her.

Mala observed him in silence. She had spent much of last night tossing and turning, the child constantly on her mind. Prakorb had told her that if she was afraid to come clean to the boy's mother, she should make amends in other ways. Uncertain, Mala wondered: If she was affectionate with the boy, would it make up for the fact that she had called him a thief? She stood face-to-face with the boy for some time, taking in his blatant fear. Then, without warning, Mala was gripped by a certain feeling that had reawakened. She trembled with excitement and, suddenly, had the scared little boy trapped inside a piece of wood outlined in his form. She was enraptured; the picture was so vivid. His upcast eyes communicated that this was a child frightened of someone who towered over him. A little human being terrified of a bigger one.

Mala's eyes lit up. This time, she would use wood with a softer flesh. The knife would have to be pointier and sharper than before so that this wood child could express itself with nuance. She could see every little detail, anticipate every little step.

But she would have to be very careful with this one: the wood would be softer, the knife sharper. One slip and the blade could easily plunge into the child's flesh.

THE ATTENDANT

THREE MORE HOURS REMAIN BEFORE I'LL BE LET OUT. I fear I won't be able to wait until then. My body might fail in the minutes to come. Other than my eyes, which glance up and down, and my right arm and hand, I haven't moved any other part of my body for over two hours. I should honestly show up for work with just my head and my right arm, leaving the rest of my body to go and do as it pleases in the outside world—do these things intensely, freely, to the best of its ability.

A body cannot survive sitting still in a confined area forever, so my limping heart tells me. Since I have legs capable of walking and running several kilometers at a time, and arms and hands fit to do tens or hundreds of thousands of things, isn't it a shame to leave them idle? And then there are my ears, my poor ears that should get to hear something, anything, with more significance than simple two-word commands, repeated over and over, bouncing only between numbers one and eight . . . The words "first floor," "fifth floor," "fourth floor," "seventh floor"—these words in and of themselves have as much meaning as the dirt under my nails, and that meaning is gone in the blink of an eye. Apart from these two-word instructions, my ears hear only deformed conversations, sometimes without a beginning, some-times without an end, and sometimes without either. But I listen—I *have* to listen. And why is that, when I should be able to listen to what I want to listen to and have the right to avoid everything else? Is it true or an illusion that I have that right, a right that I've been deprived of?

DURING THE MONSOON season, our ears could pick up the sound of storm winds over a hundred *rais* away. The rustling of wild salacca leaves served as the vessel for the sound, sending a warning signal that a storm was com-ing. In that moment, we would be on high alert, tense down to every pore. We would sprint home as if there were no tomorrow, the fatigue from the day's work in the fields forgotten like it had been wrung out of our limbs. As my little sister and I would run ahead of the pack, our mother would yell from behind, telling us what to put away and do when we got home, and how. The house was far from the fields, but we would run without stopping. Each time, our parents probably prayed that the storm would bypass us or wouldn't be severe enough to blow the crops to the ground and cause damage. But my sis-ter and I found it fun, although we would be dead tired. The wind might arrive first, followed by the rain, or they might arrive together at once, but not a single time did my sister and I ever reach our house before at least one of them hit, run as we did with all our might. Gray clouds would move swiftly from the west. Looking up, I used to think they resembled curtains being drawn over the sky. My sister liked to pretend that she was the one pulling the curtains. She would wait for the clouds to move a lit-tle ahead of us, and I would end up having to drag her along. The raindrops carried along by the storm winds were huge and fell with force. As they lashed down on us, we would feel the sting, urging us to run faster, until we arrived at our destination. I desperately want to run. If I get to, I promise this run will be like no other in my life. I will pour all my energy into it, go as far as possible, as fast as possible, wearing myself out like never before, letting my mouth get so parched it tastes bitter. Every part of my body would join forces solely for this run. My arms would be rejuvenated, as well as my legs, my blood, and my heart. Every part of my body would come alive so that I could run, run on a path of my own choosing, run far and wide. I want to run without ever turning back. Please, don't let me run only to have to turn back. I'm not an elevator door that opens only to close again, nor am I an elevator user who steps in only to step out—oh, somebody help me, help me be able to run far and wide. Yes, it ought to be far *and* wide.

SPACE IS TIGHT in the elevator, too tight for running or even walking. In such a confined space, one is meant to stand. Considering its shape, the elevator is nothing more than a coffin for the living. People zip into the elevator, all of them with energy in their steps. I get a glimpse of them before they turn their bodies around behind me and face the doors, which close from both sides. Then they stand still and utter their two-word commands at my back. Lifting my right arm, I press the button of the requested floor and watch the green light move through the numbers, flashing upward, one, two, three, four, five, six, seven, eight; flashing downward, eight, seven, six, five, four, three, two, one. When the elevator doors open, the living humans step out and in. I get a quick look at them from the front, and a quick one from the back. The elevator doors shut, and then again come the commands, jabbing me in the back as I sit motionless in my chair, forcing my right hand to rise up and press . . . The more time passes, the more heavy-handed, and pointed, those two words become. When the voices dig into my back, I feel excruciating pain. Who could tolerate sitting still, allowing pain to be inflicted on them time and time again, endlessly? The living humans have no idea that they're hurting me. Of course the ones that do the hurting don't feel the pain; the victims are the ones that bear it. And how long do I have to wait until the former are the ones that suffer, so they will stop hurting me? Or do I have to turn into a baby chick before they realize what it's like to hurt somebody, to be the ones in pain?

I KNEW THAT it was suffering, condemned to spin around like that, unable to stop. After wasting a lot of time, I discovered a way to help, which was to curl my index finger into the shape of a hook and grab it by the neck. But after some time, the symptoms would return—the twisted neck, the frozen eyes, the running in circles. The poor baby chick was attached to me, following me around constantly, and I don't know if what came to pass was the chick's misfortune or mine.

The seizures the chick endured became less and less frequent, and I thought it would soon be cured. We were together all the time; I never let it out of my sight. So whenever its neck started to contort, right before it started running in circles, I would rush over and grab its little neck with my hooked finger, a task I had to execute quickly if I wanted to prevent the symptoms from taking hold.

My chick was by my side even during meal times and when I went to the toilet. When I slept, it would huddle in a cardboard box next to me. When I went out to work in the fields, it would wander near my feet, constantly moving as they were, which meant that I nearly crushed it to death on several occasions. But then, in the blink of an eye, its fate took an ill turn all over again. As I was swinging my hoe toward the ground, destiny whispered to the poor chick and summoned it under the blade. Its left leg and a bit of its wing were sacrificed to this cruel fate. My good intentions rebuffed, I felt frustrated and wondered why I had made any effort at all. I caught myself thinking: What was the point of this chick's existence? Its life was nothing but struggle; straight out of the eggshell, it was stricken with the strange seizure disorder. Its cries made me want to dig a grave and get it over with.

The following day, I went out to the fields without the chick. It stayed at home alone, withering in the cardboard box, where I'd left some rice and water in little cups. Out in the fields, I was in a foul mood, finding fault with everyone and everything. It didn't help that I felt tired and hot. My obligation to the chick, which wasn't even supposed to have lasted this long, was now getting dragged out. What was more, I didn't like having to take on a burden that reeked of pity like this. I had never felt so tired and hot as I did that day—those conditions make it so easy for abject thoughts to plant themselves in people's minds. I even resented my little sister, who was sitting comfortably in a classroom. When the sun was directly overhead, I headed home without waiting for anyone, vowing to myself that as soon as I washed my face and ate my lunch, I would reserve the bamboo daybed under the mango tree for myself until two in the afternoon. When I got home, I immediately heard a scraping noise. It persisted in frequent intervals as I stood there listening. Soon it occurred to me to go look in the cardboard box. The rice grains had spilled all over the place, and the entire bottom of the box was damp. The chick, neck crooked and eyes frozen wide, was struggling with its remaining leg to kick and scratch its way in a circle. I hooked my index finger around its neck, tending to it for a while before the seizure finally stopped. It let out a raspy cry and then lay still, eyes half-shut, cradled in the palm of my hand. Its condition appeared to have worsened. I couldn't say how I felt in that moment, but I wondered for what purpose this chick had been born.

Under the mango tree, I lay back on the daybed, nestling the chick on my chest.

I was fed up . . . I wanted to kill it . . . but I pitied it.

I fell asleep for over an hour, instinctively waking up when it was time to go back to the fields for the afternoon. I sat up, completely forgetting that the chick could tumble off my chest. But in fact, it wasn't there. When I leaned over to look on the ground, I saw it lying there, its beak clamped onto the edge of a sheet of corrugated iron beneath the daybed, its body jerking so persistently that the sharp edge had sliced into the corners of its mouth. Its right leg was digging, leaving scratch marks on the ground. Four or five fire ants had found their way to its eyelids and the bleeding corners of its mouth. I looked at it for a short while and then got up and went inside the house. I picked out an old black work shirt too ratty to be worn. When I returned to the mango tree, the chick was in the same state as before. I spread the shirt out on the daybed, picked the chick up, brushed the ants off it, and carefully set it down on the cloth. Bending over, I observed the convulsing body up close and stared into the little eyes for a while before straightening myself up and folding one side of the shirt over the chick. I made a tight fist with my right hand and started counting, my eyes focused on the lump under the cloth; it twitched lightly, a bit like a beating heart. Then I suddenly felt so depleted that I had to unclench my fist, peel the cloth open, and hook my finger around the chick's neck until its spasms stopped. Right then, my parents walked by, their path leading in my direction. They were already heading back out to the fields. My mother looked at me and smiled, amused. For the past few days I'd been so preoccupied with the chick that I must have seemed ridiculous. I watched my parents as they walked off into the sweltering sun. I would soon follow them.

I folded the cloth over again and pounded. The first time, a squeal snuck through. I pounded twice more, and then stopped—it appeared to be enough. I grabbed the bundle of cloth and headed for the fields, my hoe on my shoulder.

Who believes me when I say that I did it to put the chick out of its misery? I was the one suffering from having to lay hands on it. Isn't it twisted? When I hurt others, I'm the one that suffers; when others hurt me, I'm the one that suffers again. I stopped hurting others because I don't want to suffer anymore. But why do they continue hurting me? How long must I wait for them to stop?

NONE OF THE living humans want to go to the fourth floor, so I don't know what time it is or how much longer I have before I can escape. Other than looking up and down and raising my right arm and hand to press a button and then dropping them back down, I haven't attempted to move the other parts of my body to see if they still function. I should honestly come to work with only my head and my right arm. My legs are strong; my body is strong, a farmer's body built for physical labor. The world has farmers, and I'm a good farmer. But right now I'm an elevator attendant, even though such a job shouldn't exist in this world. Is it so troublesome to lift your hand up and press a button that they have to pass this task off to someone else, someone who could do so many other things? If I had been born with only a head and an index finger, this job would be suitable for me. It's a shame I'm really about to be left with only those two parts. The rest of me is slowly dying . . . Soon enough everything will probably end up the way it ought to.

But now I want to find out how long I have before I'm let out. The elevator opens on the first floor: I see the fried chicken stand, a kid stuffing a drumstick into his mouth . . . The elevator opens on the fifth floor: I see a shopgirl resting her arm on a stack of bras, talking to a man . . . The elevator opens on the sixth floor: I see a group of middle-aged women sitting around a *suki* hotpot, sharing a good laugh as they lean in and ladle . . . The elevator opens on the eighth floor: I see a shopboy napping, draped over a loudspeaker, and next to him three men standing there looking at televisions . . . The elevator opens on the seventh floor: I see the concession stand with popcorn and the cinema box office, but not a soul in sight . . . The elevator opens on the second floor: I see a young couple staring into each other's eyes over cups of coffee . . . The elevator opens on the third floor: I should see the girl behind the beverage counter, but a group of men is blocking my view . . . The elevator opens on the fourth floor—at last. I steal a look at one of the clocks in the timepiece store: in less than an hour, I will be free to go. But I haven't tried to wiggle the other parts of my body to see if they still work. I hope they haven't gone and died on me, especially when my heart hasn't stopped and is now begging to leave. I so painfully want to escape, to shoot out of this place like an arrow.

Only those completely ruined by exhaustion would want to sit still and not even move a finger. I would find no joy in such immobility unless my muscles burned with pain and my legs couldn't take another step. I've sat immobile for so long; I've sat in misery for too long, and I don't want to sit any longer. My heart is still beating, and I want to completely wear myself out—completely, not moderately or momentarily. It wouldn't be right to spend one's entire life idle and then mobilize only for a momentary burst of energy. It would make me happy to exert myself to the limit for as long as possible, and it would make me happier still to then rest for a short time.

I LUGGED A bushel of cassava roots on my shoulders, its weight bearing down on me. I could barely shuffle my feet, my legs feeling like they might give at any point, as I consoled myself with the fact that this was my last haul.

When I finally reached the bottom of the wooden ramp leading up to the bed of the ten-wheeler truck, I rallied, trotting up the incline. The man I had to pass the bushel to was very high up because the cassava was piled past the top of the truck's grated wooden frame. I gathered whatever strength remained in me, bent a little at the knees, and thrust the bushel up as far as I could. As it was pulled from my hands, I felt as though all my energy had been hauled away with it, and I just let myself drop down from the ramp and collapse on the ground with the others.

One by one, we got up as the sun started to disappear. The bare land was strewn with scraps of tapioca plants. Large clumps of soil that had been dug up with the tubers were left upturned all over the fields. All of these cast long, neat shadows to the east. We scattered in different directions before daylight vanished, leaving the fully loaded truck quietly parked on that empty tract of land.

That evening a horn sounded from a distance. I bounded down from the house and ran toward the source of the honking, which was followed by the revving of an engine. As I stepped onto the road, waiting on the side, I spotted the cassava truck turning up from the top of the fields, and I could make out people's heads, appearing like dark shadows on top of the heaping mound of tubers. When the ten-wheeler drew near, the crew on top of the pile of roots leaned out to look at me and had a good laugh. I laughed back, realizing that I was the last to show up. But then instead of stopping, the driver accelerated, driving the truck right past me and kicking up a cloud of dust. I had my mouth open mid-laugh and nearly didn't get it closed in time, and I had to struggle to open my eyes. The others had a hoot at my expense. The truck parked about fifteen meters ahead. I stood there, trying to calm down, waiting until the dust had settled a bit before I walked over. Glancing down at my soiled shirt and pants, I wanted to cry. I didn't even have to think about my hair, which I'd made an effort to wash and style with oil. When I reached the truck, I yelled at the driver, who was my foreman. He sat there shaking with laugher and refused to gratify me with a response. All I could do was climb on top of the cargo to join the rest of the crew. Seeing me up close, they laughed even harder. I'd gotten so dressed up, no wonder I was the last to show, one of them teased.

Hardly anything was visible now that dusk was upon us. The truck switched on its lights and set off once again. To make room, I dug out a small space in the mound of roots to lower myself into. I was still mad at the others for another half hour or so, but eventually I relented and started chatting and joking with them. Crawling along the bumpy dirt road, the truck took nearly an hour to reach a paved street. Even though it was dark by then, the air was still heavy with heat. Only when the truck had gained some speed and the breeze started blowing was it a pleasant ride up there.

As a child, I always dreamed of cruising on top of one of these heaping loads of tapioca roots. My mother and father and the other adults wouldn't let any of the kids sit there. Back then, I could only imagine what it would be like to sit so high up. Those lucky riders could probably see far into the distance and could tell where everybody's farm was all along the way. They could most likely see the roof of every house. Especially when I thought about the truck going fast, I could hardly wait . . . The day I was allowed to sit on top of the mountain of roots for the first time—I still remember vividly how my heart raced. I looked down over the side at my little sister, who was squirming in defiance as our father tried to shove her into the cab of the truck, where our mother was already seated. Even after I backed away to find myself a place to sit as our father climbed up, I could still hear her shrieking.

The air was starting to get cooler, and the stars in the sky were twinkling. Along both sides of the truck, there was only darkness. Only once in a while would we see lights flicker from inside isolated houses. When the breeze eventually made it too chilly, we dug away the tubers and slipped ourselves deeper among them, reclining. The roots' starchy aroma, intensified by their warmth, made for a cozy place to lie down. Now and again I happily dozed off, until the truck reached the town. The bright lights woke us up instantly; wide-eyed, we immediately started looking around at all the shops and stylish people. When the truck stopped at a red light, the women strolling along the side of the road glanced at us, then turned their noses up and refused to look our way again. Together we hooted and hollered at them before the truck continued on its way. The city girls, how pretty and how slick they were. I used to wonder, if one of those ladies became my wife, would I be able to afford her wardrobe . . . Oh, how I wanted one of those smug beauties for my own, to hold close in bed every night.

We had to ride on top of the roots for nearly four hours straight, so our legs needed stretching when we climbed down at our destination. Our foreman stuck his head out, reminding us to be back at the agreed pickup time, and then continued on alone with the truck to the sorting plant, where the roots would be sold. We were dumped in the center of town, beat as we were from the harvest, to make our own way to the local watering hole. Still, we walked over together in high spirits. Although I was stiff from being cooped up for so long, I felt happy.

IT'S PRACTICALLY TIME. The living humans are finished using the elevator. The other employees will start heading out soon. I still haven't attempted to operate the other parts of my body so that I can get up and walk out, and I want to understand why. The time for my release has come. I haven't died and I can't sit still forever. It's funny to think that I was sliding up and down all the time. I hadn't remained in place but I hadn't moved, and despite that, I'm drained. It's time for me to eat. It's time for me to rest and sleep, to recharge my energy so that tomorrow I will have the strength to come back and sit still once again . . . Oh, no, this can't be. I must be mistaken—stories like this cannot really exist.

My heart is tired. If I wait any longer, it might stop altogether. Then I probably wouldn't wonder whether or not I could move anything on my body other than my head and my right arm. If my heart were to give up, it would be pointless for the other parts of my body to continue to function. I probably wouldn't want to walk even if I could. People want to walk or move with joy . . . Regardless, I have no choice but to check the other parts of my body.

With my heart dying a slow death, I try to move the rest of me. I struggle to stand even though I have no desire to get up. I step out with legs as stiff as logs. My body feels as if it's breaking apart. With extreme effort, I walk out. I can't stay here. My heart is dying, but this place is a coffin for the living; it isn't suited for my heart.

Thus I leave, even though I don't want to leave. I don't want to eat, don't want to sleep, don't want to sit still. Really, I should leave my heart and the other parts of my body here to die, and let my head and my right hand go back to eat and sleep, to relax, as compensation for the exhaustion they had to bear . . . Ah, that would be fair, wouldn't it?

THE FINAL SECRET OF
INMATE BLACK TIGER

To my dear friend Inmate Somsak,

Unless you were pulling my leg the other day, I'm happy for you. Allow me to just say, your woman is amazing. These five years you've been behind bars, she's probably been wandering around, tirelessly searching for evidence to support your case. A woman so true is hard to come by. I have to give her serious credit. If she were mine, I'd even put her up on a pedestal and worship her like a goddess. Congratulations, old friend. You're beginning to hope, aren't you? If the evidence is persuasive, they'll set you free in no time. I've believed that you're innocent all along—I don't need to see any evidence. I can read people. You were unlucky to have been locked away for somebody else's crime, but you're lucky when it comes to women. Once they let you out, if you want, you can tell her that I admire and respect her very much.

My old friend, I am writing you this letter for two reasons. First, we may never meet again because you're about to be exonerated. Second, we may never meet again because they're about to have me executed by machine gun. I'm not a good person like you, my friend, and so it's fitting that you're going to be freed, whereas I'm going to be killed. The last two or three nights, I've been thinking about something. The closer my death looms, the more I think of it. I'm not afraid to die—death is no big deal—but my mind keeps fixating on this one woman. We're not actually particularly close, though we did see each other often. She's just your everyday prostitute, no eye-catching beauty or anything like that. In fact, I'd completely forgotten about her until just a few days ago. The story involving her, even she herself, would be insignificant if I had hope that I'd be spared or if my death were at least further away. This matter—I can't tell you about it in person because I'm too embarrassed, but I can't *not* tell you because I need your help.

I first encountered this woman at the top of my street. She appeared in a dark corner next to my local coffee shop and told me her price was five hundred baht. I turned her down immediately. Not for any particular reason, but I already had three women I was sure were AIDS-free, and I didn't want to chance it with a random streetwalker. But when I went inside the coffee shop, she followed me in and sat down with me. I was annoyed, but in a generally good mood that day. To ward off her persistence, I told her something that shut her up. I didn't think she'd believe me so I feigned a sad expression until she went away. When I told my buddies the story, we laughed so hard our jaws locked. But because she lived nearby, I later ran into her again. I thought what I'd told her that day would make her not bother me anymore. As it turned out, she headed straight toward me as soon as she spotted me, but not to offer her services. She smiled at me, greeted me nicely as if we were two people with a warm and friendly rapport. When I went inside the coffee shop, she again followed me in. No, she wasn't plying her trade. She was interested in what we had talked about the other day. When I realized what her intentions were, that she wanted to offer her sympathy, I thought I'd have a little fun so I embellished some more. From then on, even though we never sat down for a real chat again, the way she behaved toward me let me know that she was giving me her lifelong friendship. With others, she'd rush up to them and tell them her price, but with me, she'd nod with a smile, wave her hand, and openly say hello. It went on like that until I eventually got used to it and stopped giving it much thought.

My dear friend, I'm going to die soon, and you are the last friend that I have in this life. Out of all the friends I've ever had, you're the best person and the only good one. I'm writing this letter and then holding on to it. I'll give it to you either the day before your release or the day before my execution, as the case may be. I want to be sure that you'll read this letter only when there's no chance we'll ever meet again. You see, it's humiliating for me, my friend.

What I want your help with is for you to go and find that hooker. Do you remember the coffee shop at the top of my street? You said you'd been there before. Tell her that the story about the guy who got his dick cut off by his wife is a lie. Vouch for me, make her believe you. Maybe you could tell her you've showered with me. Just help me, my friend. The past two nights, I haven't been able to sleep a wink, and I'll probably die with my eyes wide open if a woman is under the impression that I don't have *that*. I'm touched by the goodness of her heart, but I can't allow her to have the wrong idea forever. Alas, if I hadn't landed in prison, one day I would have told her myself. Laugh all you want, but I hope that you will help me.

From your true friend, Inmate Black Tiger

MEN'S RIGHTS

WASU SAT IN BED, HIS HEAD BEARING DOWN ON HIS
hand. He'd never been so deep in thought. It was utterly
exhausting and excruciating. But he stayed that way until
three in the morning, when he finally dropped himself
back onto the bed. While he was physically drained, his
mind was wired and his eyes were locked open.

By the time he heard her motorbike, it was almost
five a.m. His heart pounded and he tensed, hyperalert,
on the bed. He pricked up his ears: the sound of his wife
unlocking and opening the door, pushing the motorbike inside, closing and relocking the door. Wasu glared
at her black silhouette. Against the white wall, he could
make out the fair-skinned whore's face. He sniffed—
that scent again, that suspicious fragrance. The shape
of his wife moved past the bed toward the bathroom.
She switched the light on and cracked the door open to
help her see. From there, she tiptoed back to the wardrobe. Face upturned, she appeared lost in thought as she
reached into the pockets of her pants and shirt and put
their contents on the table nearby. Wasu couldn't see her
face because she had her back to him, yet instinct told
him she was smiling. Next, she undressed and tossed

her shirt and pants into the laundry hamper. Then she unhooked her bra; her underwear was the last thing she slipped off. With her bent over, her ample hips and ass loomed conspicuously.

Wasu shut his eyes, consumed by agony. One image played over and over in his mind: his young wife having sex with another man. It was unthinkable—how could it be? Here he was, crammed in bed with their two sons; the youngest was only seven months old. How could she have the heart to do it—a new mother carrying on a secret love affair, her child not yet walking? It was beyond contempt. The five years they had shared a life together obviously meant nothing to her. He was going to kill her—he needed her dead . . . As she switched off the light and felt her way onto the bed, he lay with his eyes wide open in the dark. He caught another whiff of something, an unknown smell . . . He must take her life. He must kill her. Tomorrow, once he'd brought his older boy to school, he would drop the baby off at a friend's house. Then he would come back and kill her.

At seven a.m. Wasu got his oldest son showered and ready for school. He dressed him neatly, buttoning the boy's overalls and cuffing his socks evenly on both sides. He put formula and flat cloth diapers in a backpack. While that slut of a mother was still asleep in bed, he changed the baby, powdering him front and back and pulling on his tiny clothes—a shirt and a pair of shorts. The backpack slung on his shoulder, Wasu picked up the lounger where the baby lay. He and the children made their way to the sky-blue water truck parked outside, his older boy wearing his own school bag. Wasu then carried out his plan: he dropped his son off at school and took the baby to his friend's, knowing full well that the friend's wife would be the one to babysit.

By the time Wasu got home, he was ready to explode. The door slammed open, rousing his wife into a state of drowsy confusion. Before she had the chance to wake up fully, Wasu charged in and grabbed her by the hair, dragging her off the mattress. As she shrieked, he slapped her in the mouth until her voice died down. On the floor next to the bed, he kicked her and kicked her. She cowered and moaned and tried to crawl away. Once she regained her footing, she rushed toward the bathroom and tried to shut the door and lock herself in, but he pursued her—and he was fast. This time she screamed at the top of her lungs, mouth stretched open, crying for help. She struggled with everything she had, as if she knew he wouldn't stop until she was dead. She pushed, she kicked, she did anything she could to prevent his access to her body. One of her hands managed to take hold of the mop standing in the corner of the bathroom. Without hesitation, she tried to hit him with it, but he blocked the blow, seized the mop for himself, and smashed her face with it. Blood poured out. Out of fight, she dropped to the floor, slumped over the squat toilet, her face covered in red. Wasu, too, was panting by this point, but when he pictured her having sex with another man, he kicked her again. And again and again.

This time, Wasu really was spent, but his wife was still breathing. Seeing the shape she was in, he decided to stop the beating there. He forbade her from going to work from then on—she was to stay home and take care of the children, and that would be it. If he ever caught her cheating again, he would bury a knife in her gut.

But when Wasu returned home again after picking up the baby, his wife was gone, as were her clothes and the motorbike.

Wasu realized that he was responsible for everything now. Every day he had to be out driving the truck, delivering salt water to multiple shrimp farms. By the time he managed to fill each day's orders, it was inevitably after dark. He didn't get home until nearly eight p.m., exactly when his wife would be leaving for work. This had been their routine: She looked after the baby during the day and Wasu took over at night. Their older boy hitched a ride with him on the truck every morning and rode home from school on the back of his mother's motorbike . . . This harmony had now collapsed. Wasu was lost, unable to think his way out of the situation. He couldn't afford to hire a nanny, not that he wanted his family to be raised that way anyway. But he had to find a solution, seeing that he couldn't very well quit his job to take care of the children. His only option was to find his wife and drag her back, by the hair if he must—and fast. The problem was, he had no idea where she was hiding— or who the other man could be.

Wasu emptied the basket he had been using for the baby's clothes and diapers and put the infant's lounger in it instead. He carried the basket out to the truck, secured it to the seat with a rope, loaded what he thought necessary into the vehicle, and, with the baby propped against his shoulder, did a final inspection of the house. The various neighbors, curious about the recent events, stuck their heads out. Word about the beating had already gotten around, so all of them were eager to know what had caused the outburst. Wasu was willing to indulge them. He shut his front door and walked over, cradling the baby in his arms.

"Would you mind keeping an eye on the house, Iad? I might not make it back until after dark," Wasu said.

"Hey, Ratom, this morning—what happened? Why'd you have to lay hands on her?"

"Iad," Wasu frowned, "as you know, I changed my name a long time ago. I thought a new name would improve my fortune, but my life is more cursed than ever. Fon, my wife, has run off with her lover." He swallowed and licked his parched lips.

The neighbor, Iad, exclaimed with her hand on her heart, "My goodness! How could she? The baby's not even weaned. And who's this other man? Where's he from, Ratom?"

Wasu scowled at her, shaking his head. "I'm off. I'm going to find her and bring her back."

Shortly after Wasu, then known as Ratom, had been hired for his current job, he and his friend had gone to see a monk to request a new name for him. The holy monk had told them that that particular name should have been eliminated ages ago. Being called "Ratom"— "Misery"—he was destined to be unlucky forever. The monk renamed him "Wasu." He'd made sure everyone he knew was aware of the change, yet few people bothered to adapt to it. That was probably why his life hadn't improved at all.

Wasu went to his employer to ask for time off, again with the baby nuzzled up against his chest. With a look of torment and tears welling up in his eyes, he explained his predicament: how his wife had been unfaithful and run away with her lover. Later, at three thirty in the afternoon, he went to pick his son up from school. That done, he was free for the rest of the day. But the search for his wife . . . it was like he was in the dark and couldn't find his way. Where was he supposed to start looking and how, when he didn't even know the degenerate's name? Wasu's wife, Namfon, was only twenty-two years old. She had given birth to their first child at merely seventeen. She had abandoned her hometown in Chantaburi to move to Chonburi with him so he could look for a job. He found employment as a saltwater truck driver, while she stayed home taking care of their son—the furniture she'd begged him to buy on installment, piece by piece, keeping her perfectly happy. An obedient wife, she rarely left the house and never exhibited any behavior that caused him to worry. And then, out of nowhere, what dark force caused it all to come crashing down? His boss's wife asked Wasu whether Namfon had had her tubes tied after the birth of their second child. Yes, as his wife had decided, she had. Wasu was then told that women who had had the procedure developed an elevated sex drive. It had never occurred to him that this could be the reason. But it was possible, wasn't it? His wife had turned into a slut because of her sterilization.

How bleak and full of suffering the world was. Wasu felt like he was sinking deeper and deeper all the time. He had never faced such a crisis in his entire life. When he pictured the future, he could see how his life would be turned upside down; nothing would ever be the same. He would no longer be like those around him. He'd been robbed of his vitality. His spirit had been broken. He'd lost the will to work, to see friends, to chat with anyone, to do anything at all. He'd run out of strength, of hope.

But the neighbors weren't buying the sterilization theory.

"She was born that way. As long as she stayed at home and didn't meet anyone, she kept herself in line. But as soon as she started working and got to meet and talk with new people a little, she showed her true colors."

Perhaps they were right; Wasu allowed himself to be swayed. He had unknowingly married a slut, the kind to really spread her love around. That was why it wasn't long before she acted out. Such innate characteristics weren't something easily uprooted. But regardless of the cause, the consequence was unfair to him. Their two sons—his wife had to share responsibility for them. So he had to find her. He was going to drag her back, one way or another.

Later that night, Wasu crept out of the house, leaving his two sleeping children alone. Since it wasn't too far, he decided to walk. Once out of the housing development, he made his way up the main road until he saw the gas station where his wife worked. Instead of going straight in and asking, he hid behind a tree, using it to shield himself from the light. He stared unblinkingly at the station, waiting for her to appear, even though he knew too well the serious nature of her injuries. But he hoped for the off chance that she would come to ask for the night off. For close to an hour, he continued his stakeout, despite knowing deep down it was utterly pointless. Maybe she'd already come by that afternoon. Or perhaps she didn't need to ask for leave—she'd probably just decided to quit and go live somewhere else with her lover. That had to be the story. He would never see his wife's face again.

Wasu walked home, barely aware of the motion of his own body. It seemed that his life had sunken to an all-time low. He realized that there was no justice in this world. At random, a person could be forced to endure hardship all alone. Yes, that was the truth. This was what reality looked like. He saw it now, with painful clarity.

The next morning, Wasu repeated the same routine. He dressed his older son, bathed and powdered the baby, and they all climbed into the truck. With any luck, he would make some headway on finding his wife today. He dropped his son off at school, but after that he found himself in the same situation: at a loss as to where to even begin searching for his wife. In the end, he drove over to his friend's house. He knew that Boonleua wouldn't be in: he and this friend of his had the same job—both were water-truck drivers, and they never made it home before dusk. Wonpen, Boonleua's wife, still had no children even though she was several years older than Namfon; she did, however, like looking after children, and wanted very much to have her own. Whenever something came up with Wasu's two boys, he could rely on Wonpen to look after them. She was their godmother, and every time she saw Wasu lifting the kids down from the truck, she never failed to welcome them with a smile.

Looking at his friend's wife, Wasu felt his own misfortune even more acutely. Truckers like he and Boonleua were frequently scheduled for long-distance trips, which meant that Wonpen often spent the night alone, and the woman wasn't even tied down by the obligations that came with having children. After almost ten years of living that way, why hadn't she allowed herself to stray like Namfon? He should have taken a woman like her for a wife. Just look at her—she loves his children even more than their real mother! The thought thrust him even deeper into despair, and he began to sob. Wonpen rubbed Wasu's back and shoulders for a long while trying to console him, looking like she too might cry.

Between venting his grief and speculating wildly, Wasu ended up spending the entire morning with his friend's wife. He made to leave several times, intending to go search for his wife, but always wound up sitting back down. He eventually departed at three thirty, leaving the baby with Wonpen.

Wasu went to pick up his older son from school—the boy was waiting for him out front—and now he had to double back to pick up the younger one. Yes, the back and forth seemed like a lot of trouble, but he was willing to do it. As it turned out, his timing was impeccable—he couldn't have planned it better. There was his wife! The shock left him numb: Namfon was sitting by herself inside Boonleua's truck, which was parked on the roadside. In that instant, everything became clear as day. He understood now. He didn't have far to go before he reached Boonleua's house. Wasu pulled over in front of the truck and stormed over to his wife. Their son turned and saw his mother, so he jumped out as well.

Namfon was sitting inside the other truck, stunned. Once she snapped out of it, she quickly reached over and locked both doors. Their son, running, beat Wasu to the truck. Clutching the footboard, the boy threw his head back and begged and begged his mother to open the door for him. Because she didn't, his hollers soon turned into wails.

Wasu stood in the front of the truck, glaring at his

wife. His whole body trembled with rage; he tried to force it still. He knew he'd already given her the beating she deserved, but he still had to settle the score with her lover, whose identity he now knew. The only thing was, her infidelity had cut him so deeply that he wanted to give her one more good, hard slap just for the satisfaction. He ought to find a stick that fit nicely in his hand and smash the front of Boonleua's truck in and yank that no-good wife of his out by her hair—that was what he should do. But he found himself not wanting to go through with it. The urge to hurt her began to dissipate and slowly become consumed by another desire. Such a knee-jerk reaction would just get in the way of his other plans.

Namfon was paralyzed with fear. Her face was covered in green bruises and misshapen from the swelling of her right jaw, and she had a bandage on her left cheek. Still, she met Wasu's eyes defiantly as she held her breath, waiting for his next move.

But then Wasu simply returned to his own truck. He waited until he saw Namfon open the door for their son and let him climb in before he started the engine and drove off.

At Boonleua's, the husband and wife were busy packing clothes and other items into a duffle bag. Wasu walked in, perfectly calm, calling out a greeting as soon as he stepped inside.

"I've been over here a lot recently, and I haven't seen you at all."

Boonleua paused, studying his friend for a minute. "Pen told me. That's rough. Let me know if I can help with anything."

Wasu laughed. "I was thinking about it. But I don't want to impose."

"What is it?" Boonleua asked as he fussed with his travel bag. When he didn't hear a reply, he stopped what he was doing and looked at his friend.

As their eyes locked, Wasu's anger flared up again. Boonleua was supposed to be his best friend. They had long been eating and drinking buddies. They had sworn their lifelong allegiance to one another. They had known each other for over a decade. They were from the same hometown. They spoke the same language. They had helped each other out more times than he could count. Wasu bristled with resentment. He wasn't the type to take this kind of insult lying down. He should lunge at Boonleua's throat and fight him to the death. This was an act of war, an affront that warranted an equally grievous act of revenge.

Boonleua searched his friend's bloodshot eyes for either anger or sorrow. Finding only ambiguity, he forced himself to remain calm and not overreact.

"All set," Wonpen said. She zipped up the bag and carried it over to the door.

Boonleua followed his wife's movements, staring at the bag a few seconds before speaking up.

"This trip is going to be a long one. I'll probably be gone several days."

"Go right ahead." Wasu's eyes were on Wonpen. The image of her picking up his baby and resting him on her shoulder had an immediate calming effect on the father of two. "Don't worry, I'll look after things here for you."

Boonleua tensed up at once. He turned left then right, his eyes shifting restlessly.

"Why haven't you left yet? It's past six!" Wonpen said to her husband.

"It's all right. I can be a little late."

Wasu smirked and turned toward Wonpen. "I have to trouble you a bit at the moment, Pen."

"Of course, it's no trouble at all. Don't think anything of it! It's not a big deal, it's me you're talking to after all."

"I should be able to figure everything out in a few days. My older son shouldn't be a problem. The younger one, I'll try taking him to my mother's. See if she can manage."

"There's no hurry," Wonpen said. "Just deal with whatever you need to deal with first."

"Thank you. Regardless, I need to think of a solution as quickly as possible."

Boonleua was visibly agitated. "Have you picked up your son yet, Ratom? School let out a while ago."

Wasu glared at him. "Damn you, Leua! You know that name is cursed. You drove me to that monk to get my name changed. You of all people should know better, but, still, you refuse to use my new name. You're doing it intentionally—I know it!"

"I know what you're thinking," Boonleua said, fuming too now. "It doesn't matter what your name is. *It's* not the problem. *You* are."

"What is it about me? What is it? What?" Wasu got loud. "Don't forget that you were the one who said it— how I was cursed by the name Ratom. And now you're taking it back? *You're* the one who's making my life so shitty. The fact that you were able to do what you did to a friend—you're not even human."

"Let me tell you something," Boonleua responded

even louder. "It's not me, it's you. Everything that's happening—just think about it—it's all your fault."

Wonpen was horrified. Her eyes flitted back and forth between the two men as she struggled to understand what was happening.

Wasu was furious but confused. Boonleua's words made no sense—maybe he was being evasive to try and get himself out of a bind. Or perhaps Boonleua still thought he was too stupid to have caught on.

"Be straight with me, Boonleua. There's no point mincing words. Or do you want me to say what you've done?"

Boonleua bit his tongue, suddenly remembering that his wife was standing right next to him.

Wasu snorted, jerking his chin to one side.

Wonpen used their silence as an opportunity to say to her husband, "Why don't you two clear this up later? Weren't you in a hurry to leave?"

Boonleua looked at his wife and then turned to Wasu. "We're not going to settle this today. Why don't you go home?"

"Why don't *you* go to work?" Wasu sneered.

Boonleua clenched his jaw. "Get the hell out! Otherwise, you and me, let's take this outside."

"That's enough. This has gone too far!" Wonpen, who couldn't stand watching from the sidelines any longer, intervened by inserting herself between them.

But Boonleua was quick to shove her aside. He pointed a finger at his wife's face and said, "This isn't women's business. Take the kid outside. Go!"

Wonpen shot him an indignant look and then swung her head and walked out. Boonleua waited until his wife made it to the bench under the tamarind tree across the road. Then he turned to face Wasu.

"If you touch my wife, you're a dead man," Boonleua growled.

"You son of a bitch." Wasu got right in his face. "Now do you get it? You can't stand the thought of your wife having an affair with your friend. What about me? How could you do it? Why did you do it? How could you?"

Wasu finally snapped. He jumped at Boonleua, who already had his guard up. They threw punches, tangling themselves together, but suddenly froze: Boonleua was holding a kitchen knife in his hand. Outmaneuvered, Wasu ended up on the floor, back against the wall. Both were breathing heavily. The knife, pointed and gleaming, had restored a sense of calm.

"Listen to me, Ratom," Boonleua said finally. "I did it because you did it to me first. You stole my Moddang."

"Moddang . . ." The name fell out of Wasu's mouth. Suddenly, everything clicked. Moddang—it was because of Moddang. Oh—when had he slipped up? How had Boonleua found out?

Boonleua tossed the knife onto the table and dropped himself into a chair. "Let's call it even."

"Those things are hardly even, Boonleua. Moddang is *that* kind of woman—anybody's free to take her anywhere they want. But Namfon, she's my wife, the mother of my children—two of them! You've taken it too far. I swear I've never even thought about making a move on your wife, and I've had plenty of opportunities, believe me. All I did was fool around a bit with your whore—that's it."

"She wasn't a whore!" Boonleua shouted. "Moddang was just a kid. She lost her virginity to me—she belonged to me. She wasn't just one of *those* women anyone can pay to take around as they please. I was serious about her. It wasn't just a fling."

Wasu sighed, exhausted. He didn't know what else to say. Both men were still for a long time. Although neither of them expressed it, they did share one sentiment: each felt an enormous weight lifted off his chest. While they didn't yet know how to resolve this debacle, at least they now knew how it had come about. That alone made the impossible appear less so. And because each of them was eager to downplay what he thought was his own fault in the matter, the problem at hand shrank in significance.

Boonleua was the first to speak up. "Let's get out of here, toss back a few drinks, and get a bite to eat."

The hot sun had largely retreated for the evening, and the scene, the light at this hour, was easy on the eyes. Under the tamarind tree, Wonpen and Namfon sat side by side; the baby was snuggled against his mother's chest, while his big brother entertained himself by drawing in the sand. Wasu and Boonleua limped out of the house, dragging their heavy feet over toward the women.

"So," Wonpen said, "you could only work things out through violence? Where are you headed now?"

"We're going to find us a few drinks," Wasu replied. He smiled at Wonpen and glanced quickly at Namfon.

Boonleua, too, peeked at Namfon, but he didn't look at Wonpen at all. He threw his arm around Wasu's shoulders, and the two walked off.

The women stared after them. Wonpen grumbled about Wasu. She thought that now that he had found his wife, he should have talked things out with her. But instead, he just went and walked away. Namfon, meanwhile, sat lifelessly on the bench. Her face was badly bruised, her eyes on the verge of tears.

"So, what do you say?" Wasu said. "Should we just trade or what?"

Boonleua's feet stopped. He stepped back from Wasu and threw his hands aggressively on his hips. "We've already traded Moddang for Namfon that's done. Pen's out of the question."

"You just said that you were serious about Moddang, and it's obvious that you're pretty indifferent toward Pen."

"That's no longer the case. Moddang became a whore the moment she let you take her out."

"Well then, have the woman choose for herself."

"That's my wife you're talking about." Boonleua was beginning to lose his temper again. "She's not going to choose anybody because she's already chosen me."

"Oh, she'll choose—if she finds out you're having an affair with my wife."

Boonleua glared at him, with nothing to say in response.

"All right, all right. Let's go grab that drink." Wasu wrapped his arm around Boonleua's shoulders. "We can discuss this another time. Anyway, in the end Pen might choose you regardless, but you've got to give her the choice, you know? After a certain point, you have to allow women the honor of choosing."

Boonleua disagreed, but didn't respond. The two continued walking down the road, linked at the shoulders.

WITHIN THESE WALLS

THE FEELING FIRST HIT ME WHEN I WOKE UP ONE morning. I was lying by myself in our huge bed, which felt strangely empty. My husband was in the hospital. I could still see his face: mangled beyond recognition, swollen like a soccer ball. It had been three days. He probably wasn't going to make it. It seemed like I was trying to make myself feel something, anything at all. My heart sank—wasn't I the least bit sad? Or did I not yet believe that he was really dying? That certainly wasn't the case—I believed it. Even yesterday, when I stood there looking at him, it was like he was already dead.

My heart sped up as I scanned the bedroom. It was full of signs of him. These beige walls had once been white. Maybe four or five years ago, my husband and I had decided to repaint the room a different color. He thought white was too bright, and I agreed. But when I'd suggested a pale green, which I liked, he'd dismissed me, saying absolutely not, that he didn't think green was nice at all, and then he'd chosen beige. It wasn't as if I couldn't take a hint—all he needed to say was that beige was nicer than green.

And that was that. It was a minor thing, after all, choosing a wall color. It wasn't exactly complicated. And

I'd told myself that, since I loved him, I ought to go along with his wishes.

I should hurry up, shower, and get dressed to go be by his side at the hospital. He wasn't dead yet, and in what little time that remained, I should be doing everything I could for him. But hard as I tried to motivate myself, I couldn't get out of bed . . . What could I really do for him anyway? He couldn't even breathe without a machine! Me on the other hand, I needed to figure out what was wrong. Wasn't it crazy that the issue about the wall color had been bothering me this entire time? I wanted to tell myself that it didn't mean anything, that it was just something random I remembered that happened to spring to mind.

I sat up, my body trembling all over. I suddenly ripped off the blanket, bunched it up, and hurled it at the vanity, knocking over all my cosmetics. The perfume bottles rolled off the table and shattered on the floor, filling the whole room with their stench. I burst into tears, my anger mounting as I looked around the room.

I'd lived with him here for eight years, ever since we got married. Now he was close to dying, or might already be dead for all I knew. I didn't know if I should laugh, be upset, or pity myself: every single thing in this house was just like that wall color—they were all things that *he* liked, because they were nicer, better, or more appropriate than anything I liked.

I jumped out of bed and grabbed two lipsticks. I pulled the caps off, twisted the tubes, and started scribbling all over those perfect beige walls. Of all things, I really wanted to understand why he'd felt the need to insist on beige. Why did he care which color was "nicer"? He knew I preferred green, so why couldn't he have chosen something *I* liked for once? He never paid attention to what I wanted. He probably didn't even realize that I had my own opinions, too. I'd married him because I wanted to live life as a couple, a team, not like I was his shadow. Look around! Every single thing in this room had his name written all over it, every single thing. I flung the stumps of lipstick away, the walls now smeared with red and magenta—his favorites, of course. The perfumes were making me lightheaded, and I collapsed on the floor, sobbing hysterically.

By the time I managed, with difficulty, to calm myself down, it was almost nine in the morning. I tried to think clearly as I got up to go to the bathroom: Was I losing my mind? Maybe I'd cracked. Throughout our eight years of marriage, we'd never had any problems or fought at all. My husband was the top aide to a politician who belonged to a powerful cohort in our province. In my opinion, my husband was even more well-connected than his boss. Everybody wanted access to him because, with a snap of his fingers, he could arrange for their children to be admitted to the best public schools, help procure IDs for people who had lost theirs or never had one to begin with, and even manage to have deeds issued to people who had never owned land.

Bitterness started seeping into my heart. I'd never asked myself whether or not I liked the way we lived. Why hadn't his dealings bothered me before? I could only laugh. How could they? A woman like me getting to rub shoulders with all the wives of the most important politicians, attending all the same social events? We all received special privileges; nepotism was to be expected, wasn't it? But how could I have lied to myself? Throughout these eight years, I'd been living in this filth all along.

I stood in front of a full-length mirror, taking a good look at myself. My hair was getting long again. I remembered how, before the accident, my husband had told me to get it trimmed, but I still hadn't done it. I wasn't going to cut my hair anymore. I liked it long, didn't I? Without makeup and jewelry, my face appeared plain and washed-out: I looked more like an average working-class woman than a moneyed lady. Digging through the bottom of my closet, I pulled out an old pair of pants and a shirt and threw them on. They smelled slightly of mothballs, but I was content because I'd picked out the outfit and bought it on my own, following my own mind and my own taste. At first glance, I almost didn't recognize the person in the mirror. But I quickly corrected myself: this here was the real me. When I was seventeen or eighteen, before I was married, this was how I used to be. My thoughts and decisions used to be all my own. Not that I was claiming to be a good judge of things, but at least I expressed my genuine self.

INSTEAD OF DRIVING my own car, I took the bus to the hospital. It was almost noon when I arrived. What I heard from the nurse shocked me: my husband was no longer in the ICU but had been transferred this morning to one of the premium rooms. I made my way to the room she'd indicated and paused in front of the door, having failed to even ask her about my husband's condition. When I went in, I saw him lying in bed, no longer using a respirator. A table in the corner of the room was packed with vases upon vases of flowers. Five visitors were already there, including his boss.

"Where have you been? Why haven't you been here looking after him?" his boss snapped. I didn't reply and simply kept my head down. "I was worried sick, especially so close to the election! I didn't sleep at all last night so I came to check on him early this morning. The doctor said Vinai's very lucky. He's out of danger now." He sighed. "I feel like a weight's been lifted off my shoulders."

While I stood there listening to him, I stared at my husband, my mind in complete disarray. My husband wasn't going to die. He really wasn't going to die, even if I could barely recognize his misshapen face.

"I'm going to take off then," the boss said. Then he leaned down and whispered to me, "I know this must be difficult for you, but you need to dress more appropriately. What will people think? Everyone knows you're Vinai's wife. Until he recovers, you're going to have to help me with the campaign. Don't ever leave the house in such a state again. It's not respectable." Then he and the others walked out.

I left the hospital around one p.m., instructing our housekeeper to stay with my husband. Feeling hungry and a bit dizzy, I walked, perhaps out of habit, into a restaurant I'd frequented with my husband because he was friends with the owner, having done the man many favors over the years. There was a long line of people waiting to order. For the first time there, I also got in line. One of the workers, after staring at me for a moment, recognized me and called me over to the front of the line. I smiled but declined his offer by looking down. There were five people ahead of me.

"Ma'am!" I heard a voice say. I looked up to find the plump face of the owner. "There's no need to wait. Please, this way, please. I went to see Khun Vinai this morning. Thank god!" Bowing and gesturing with an open palm, he insisted that I go ahead and order my food. I shook my head, telling him several times that it was all right, but he refused to relent. Eventually, I was forced to give in. He went and instructed his employee, "Look after the lady, and don't charge her," and then he walked off.

All five pairs of eyes in line glared at me. I took my food and quickly tried to pay. The worker smiled and pushed the money away, politely refusing. I tried again but was rebuffed, the gesture this time sending the bills flying onto the floor. Flustered, the employee apologized. I felt put on the spot. The scene was becoming so drawn out that the people waiting behind me looked even more irritated. All I could do was thank the employee and bend down to collect the money. As I stood back up, someone in line bumped my arm, sending my tray of food crashing onto the ground. The whole place went silent, all eyes trained on me. I was about to scream; I felt like I was losing my mind. Exasperated and in a rage, I threw the money onto the floor and stormed out of the restaurant, though I couldn't even feel my legs.

I went home, the feeling from this morning still palpable. One of our housekeepers had come into the bedroom to tidy up, but the red and magenta streaks remained untouched on the beige walls and the perfume still clung to the air. I felt drained. I slumped into a chair and found my body so limp that I didn't think I could get up to do anything ever again. My husband was not in fact going to die; he would recover. I had to keep reminding myself that he would return soon, return to our home, to his work, to serve as the politician's aide, to fill his own bank accounts and those of his boss, to pick up where he'd left off with laying the foundations for his promising future. He would certainly return; after all, he was still the same Vinai, unchanged. And I was still Vinai's wife, as I had been for eight years.

I was taken aback by something then: when I first saw my husband lying on the gurney, before the operation, from that very second, I was convinced that he was going to die. What kind of wife writes off her husband when there's still breath left in him? What kind of wife then spends that time thinking about wall paint instead of praying for her husband's very survival?

Even though I was horrified by this person kicking and screaming inside me, I was determined to get a handle on it. It was enticing, a taste of life's freedom. Yet it also terrified me so much that I shivered. It had made me indifferent toward my husband's accident, numb to the plausible death of someone I'd shared a life with. I couldn't help but hate myself, the shame rippling inside of me. What did I even want? What exactly was it that I longed for most? Over the past eight years, what had been real and what had been a lie?

The whole time we'd been together, I'd been well aware of the way our life was supposed to be. It wasn't as if I hadn't known the dirty details, and yet I'd managed to live with them, even accepted them with open arms. But what of the wall color? I'd always told myself that it was nothing, but I never forgot. It buried itself deep down, patiently waiting for a moment to reassert itself. I knew now—it came from the real me. It was my own self, which now I craved so desperately. I could no longer return to the same life.

I couldn't keep living among all this corruption. I wanted my true self back, wanted it so badly that I'd been hardened to someone's death. Could that be right? Had I really thought that I could only be myself if my husband died?

IT'S NEARLY FIVE in the afternoon when I rush out of the house. My husband's still alive. Luckily, he's still alive. He wasn't conscious this afternoon. I remember how the left side of his head had two small holes drilled into it and tubes sticking out of them. His bloated, contorted face covered in little cuts from the broken glass; both of his eyes bandaged. On the way, I pray that he not regain consciousness before I get there. A sick person wants somebody to care for him, somebody to be by his side, and that somebody is me. It's a miracle he's still alive. I'll look after him until he makes a full recovery.

And when he does, I'll discuss the wall color with him again, along with all the other things churning inside me. When that day comes, I'll know whether my true self can only exist if he's absent from my life, or if it depends only on my own resolve.

HOW A LAD FOUND HIS UNCLE
AND LEARNED A LESSON

WHAT A WONDERFUL WORLD WE LIVE IN—I'VE ALREADY
said this to myself so many times in my life, even though
a young man like me still has plenty of good years left.
No matter; in my experience I've encountered only good
things, many more than I could possibly count. But if
I had to, I wouldn't be able to think of any examples.
I'm awfully forgetful! As for the not-so-good things, I
couldn't tell you about them either, not because they've
slipped my mind, but because I've hardly endured anything of the sort. Look at my current situation: I had no
job, no prospects, and practically no place to lay my head
at night. Then, as luck would have it, someone told me
that I had an uncle I could turn to. I honestly didn't think
it was purely a matter of luck. It must have been part of
the universe's plan to make the world an even better
place, and I was going to follow that plan.

Walking in search of my uncle's house, I lugged my
bags, looking for the address I had noted down. The little town wasn't very developed, but the people seemed
kind.

I approached the first person I saw, a middle-aged
lady, and asked, "Auntie, do you know Uncle Boonsom?"

"Which Boonsom?" she asked back, probably wanting more details so she could point me in the right direction.

"My uncle owns an auto repair shop in the market."

"So go look in the market," she said, disappearing into her house.

I was about to inquire further—*And where is the market?*—but it was too late because the woman had shut the door. I'm such a slowpoke! I wanted to knock, but I didn't want to be a bother. She didn't look too happy—probably because she was concerned for me and embarrassed she couldn't help—and decided to hole up inside her house.

After that, I stopped to ask several others, but they didn't shed much more light on the situation. That made me sad. Here I was about to start a new life with my uncle, but on my first day, I'd already troubled countless people and made them worry about me. Ashamed that they couldn't help, they all closed their doors and locked themselves in. It was up to me to show them kindness first. After all, I was a stranger coming into their village and hoping to live among them. At some point down the line, I knew I'd have a chance to make it up to them.

In any case, I found my uncle's place eventually. He really did own a car repair shop in the market, just like someone had said. I estimated him to be at least fifty-five years old, but no older than sixty. We have similar features, my uncle and I, so he and my father must look a lot alike. I bet I'm the spitting image of my dad, or so I would guess—I've actually never met him—but the resemblance between my uncle and me leads me to believe as much. To my surprise, despite the fact that we look related, my uncle didn't believe that

I was his nephew. Although I explained the situation to him in great detail, he remained in denial. Finally, bystanders who thought I really was his nephew had to chime in and help talk to him. Even then, he still couldn't bring himself to fully embrace me. I heard him complain under his breath:

"I've lived on my own for this long, and no one has bothered to look after me. Now that I'm almost dead, a nephew pops up. Probably hoping for an easy inheritance."

In the end, he allowed me to stay. How nice of him to take me in—and this in spite of the fact that he still didn't believe I was his nephew. As for the inheritance or whatever, I sympathized with him: he didn't trust me, so naturally he was afraid that I would deprive his rightful nephew of what belonged to him. I was so touched by my uncle's love for his true nephew—which in fact was me—that I was almost moved to tears.

After my uncle showed me where I was to stay, I came back out to meet the mechanics who worked for him. My uncle wanted me to start working at the garage that very day. To be honest, I would rather have rested a bit, being exhausted from half a day's travel. But, you see, how could I go against the wishes of my uncle, who was so eager to teach me all he knew? I spent the rest of the day diligently learning about different types of nuts and wrenches, and became somewhat acquainted with the three mechanics. One handled paint jobs, another beat out car bodies, and the last fixed engines. I felt a little closer to the latter two because the guy who did paint work was more solitary and didn't have a lot of tasks for me. All three seemed to be good guys and consistently engaged me in conversation. They were probably concerned that I, a newcomer, would feel awkward around them. I was touched. If given the chance, I'd certainly repay them for their kindness.

After work, I showered, put on some nice clothes, and went out to meet the three mechanics at a coffee shop, as they'd suggested. They wanted to take me out to celebrate since it was my first day at the garage. I'm a lucky person like that: no matter where I go, I always manage to meet friendly people. Having left with time to spare, I strolled along, enjoying the view of the early evening sky. I cut through some fields because I thought the landscape looked nice. Reeds, some tall, some short, grew more densely as I walked on, and I thought, *Wouldn't it be nice if there was a little path?* And then suddenly, there it was, a small footpath right in front of me. This is what I mean: it seems like luck grants me whatever I wish for . . . but I think it's more than that. I started to follow the path, unable to contain my excitement over what I might come across next.

The path led me to a well and a young woman; she was dripping wet and had a sarong secured around her chest. In truth, I had heard the sounds of someone bathing from a distance, and I had had a feeling that it was a woman. At that point, I had fully emerged from behind the reeds and was staring at her. She likely already saw me, too, because I wasn't trying to be inconspicuous. I stood still, waiting for her to turn and acknowledge me, but she didn't look my way for so long I became convinced that she wasn't actually aware of my presence. Wanting to strike up a conversation, I searched for something to say but couldn't quite find the right words. Meanwhile she squatted down on three or four planks of wood and began to scrub herself. I figured she would surely notice me when she turned her attention to her left arm. But she kept playing dumb. I got bored of waiting for my cue, so I changed tack and decided to simply stand and watch, as if I were looking at a beautiful picture in a newspaper, one that I could inspect from every angle. And it was a moving picture, too. My anxiety disappeared instantly, and I was walking on air . . . The picture was certainly nice.

Suddenly I froze, scared to death, because the woman had begun screaming her head off, catching the sarong that had fallen to her waist. I also realized that my feet had been moving. But I hadn't been walking toward her but around her. Like I said, I only saw her as a picture, and I wanted to examine the different elements from every possible angle. I was face-to-face with her by then. She stared at me, her left hand now clutching the sarong over her breasts. In her other hand, she held a rope that went down into the well. She couldn't let go of either. To make a move, she would have to choose between letting the sarong or the rope fall.

"Can you help me with the water bucket?" she asked finally.

From the look in her eyes, I thought she was communicating a sense of goodwill. If I helped her with the water, I would get to see her even closer, I reasoned. I would get to pore over the drops of water on her face and body. And I would be reciprocating her goodwill. But if I remained still, merely watching, letting the scene take its natural course, she would be able to resolve the situation on her own. After all, I just happened to be standing there, and what was more, I had completely separated myself from her. She was only an image, and I a mere observer.

"Hey! If you're not going to help, then get out of here," she snapped.

My aesthetic moment vanished immediately. I rushed over to help her. Once she handed me the rope, she turned around to secure her sarong. I began hoisting up the rope and a bucket full of water.

"You're Uncle Som's nephew, right?" She was leaning against the well, which came up to her waist, her hands resting on the edge.

"Yes. Do you want me to pour the water in this other bucket?" When she nodded, I dumped the water into the bucket next to the wooden planks and turned to fetch more.

"That's enough," she protested. She walked over to the planks, squatted down, and tucked the sarong even tighter around her chest. I took her place by the side of the well. "People in this town aren't too welcoming of strangers," she said, pouring a bowl of water over herself and then lathering up with soap. I continued watching her. "A couple of months ago, a man asked to stay over at Yai's place. That night, he robbed Yai and another house, a rich family. That was just two months ago." She started rinsing off with the rest of the water. "This afternoon people couldn't stop talking about the new face in town. They thought it might be that same bastard." Pausing, she stood, grabbed a dry sarong, pulled the tube of fabric over her head, then held the front of it up with her teeth, using one hand to drape the sides over her shoulders. With her other hand, she maneuvered the wet sarong, letting it fall to her ankles. "Mai said he was going out drinking with a new guy from the garage tonight. I thought it might be you," she said once her mouth was free, the new sarong having been tucked over her chest once more. From there she picked up the cloth that was piled on the ground and wrung it out. Once done, she grabbed a white towel and put it over her shoulders.

I had barely been listening to a word she said. She was a beautiful woman, with such a natural way about her. She unabashedly bathed in front of me, chatting all the while, even though I hadn't taken in anything.

It was getting dark. A swarm of mosquitoes had begun devouring my arms. She was getting ready to head home, and I had hardly said a thing to her.

"I should be going," she said.

"Will you be here tomorrow? Maybe I could come and talk with you some more?" I rushed to ask before she left.

She scrutinized me for a long while, looking ready to sigh, and then said, "Don't bother. Go look for girls somewhere else."

"No, I'll be here again tomorrow," I insisted, blurting out, "I just want to come and watch you."

"Look, I have a husband."

I knew it—that's what she'd been thinking. But it made me happy that she was beautiful both inside and out.

"That's all right. I just want to watch you bathe, that's all."

"Do you think women like it when men watch them bathe?" She seemed annoyed, but I wasn't upset with her at all. I even liked her more. "The only reason I let you stand there and watch is because I already have a husband."

She walked off as the sky was losing its light. I watched the towel covering her shoulders slowly disappear into the dark shadows of the reeds and trees. The sound of her flip-flops slapping against her heels faded as well. I really liked her; I was determined to return the next day.

Having haphazardly made my way to the road again, I doubled back to the coffee shop to meet up with the mechanics. As soon as I arrived, I smelled alcohol in the air. My three coworkers, seated around a little table in the middle of the shop, called me over to join them. To be honest, I don't drink often, even though it gives me a pretty nice feeling whenever I do. The three of them asked me various questions about my life, but I didn't have a lot to say. This went on until we'd finished a whole bottle of liquor. I was starting to feel drunk, but my colleagues looked completely composed. I thought they were going to order another round, but Chon, the panel beater, asked for the bill and paid it himself. I realized then that I didn't have any money on me. It was all right though; I knew I'd get to treat them next time.

After we left the coffee shop, the three guys started whispering to one another, snickering. At first I thought we were going to call it a night, but Pook, the engine mechanic, said they weren't done taking me out yet.

"Where are we going?" I asked, but they only cracked up.

"You'll find out," Chon said. Then he turned to the paint repairman: "Hey, but there's no way Mama Tang has any girls as pretty as your wife." He and Pook burst out laughing. I hadn't known the paint guy was married.

"Assholes . . ." the latter grumbled. "Obviously! If my wife wasn't better looking than a whore, why the hell would I have married her?"

"Cut the bullshit, Mai. You're always bragging about how hot your wife is, but what about things in the bedroom? I bet things in that department are lousy," Pook taunted.

So the paint repairman's name was Mai. As for Chon and Pook, I'd learned their names that afternoon. The paint guy's name immediately struck me. I thought I had heard the woman by the well mention the name Mai, but I couldn't remember the context in which she brought it up. She could very well be his wife. In any case, my good spirits left me completely; I felt like a rope being pulled to the breaking point. While I was trying to recall why the young woman had mentioned the name, this Mai was boasting compromising details about his wife, even making dirty gestures. The other two were clapping and laughing their heads off. I tried as hard as I could to control my anger, but the rope finally snapped. I grabbed Mai's arm to stop him, and he turned to look at me.

Taking a deep breath, I forced out, "You shouldn't talk about stuff like that." I tried to keep my tone as even as I could, but he immediately looked furious.

"Why are you sticking your nose in this?" Chon countered. "If he wants to talk about his wife, so what? It sure doesn't bother me!" He laughed again.

"You should really go home to your wife," I told Mai.

"It's none of your concern. She's my wife; I'll talk about her however I want." He seemed like he was gearing up for a fight.

"Hey! Hey! What are you guys doing?" Pook stepped in between me and Mai. "C'mon, let's go find us some hookers."

"You already have a wife. So why do you need a whore?" I asked sternly.

"Moron," Pook spat. "The wife's a sure thing. A man can have that whenever. He can even have it later tonight when he's home. Am I right, Mai?" He nodded toward Mai but the latter was in no mood. He kept staring me down. It dawned on me then that he, too, was like a rope under strain, and I knew that as soon as it snapped, I would get beaten to a pulp because I was the one pulling it. I could either let go of the rope or keep on tugging, and I made my choice.

"You shouldn't treat your wife like that," I insisted, my tone emotionally charged this time. "Your wife's a good woman. I know she wouldn't cheat on you even if she had the chance."

"What did you say?" The other two fell silent as Mai got up in my face. "What the fuck did you just say? Who told you my wife was a good woman? That she wouldn't cheat?"

I kept my mouth shut. I had planned on telling him about the woman at the well because I had somehow become convinced that she was his wife. But I couldn't come up with the right words; I didn't want to cause her any trouble.

Mai glared at me menacingly. My silence had probably given him time to put two and two together. "Where were you earlier this evening?" he asked.

"At the well," I said, and just like that, the rope snapped. He hit me square in the chin. I didn't fall back but stumbled forward, folded over like a wuss. I'd meant to tell him more than the fact that I'd gone to the well, but I didn't have the chance. That first punch really helped: it saved me from being conscious of what followed while I was crumpled on the ground. Only a bit later did I sense that his hands and feet had stopped their assault. I could hear Mai panting.

"Son of a bitch!" he yelled. "You act like such a nice guy after putting the moves on my wife? Don't you two help him. Just leave him there. And if I find out that one of you helped him home, I'll kick the shit out of you." The voice came from farther and farther away.

I felt a foot nudge me twice.

"You shouldn't have."

I couldn't tell whose voice it was. After that, I heard a faint conversation and the sound of feet shuffling away.

Still, I managed to smile. I shouldn't have judged the paint repairman so harshly. He obviously loves his wife and guards her jealously. He really is a good guy just like I had believed in the beginning. I'm truly sorry to have misunderstood. And his wife's so lovely. He's probably gone to her now. Wait until tomorrow when I go to the well—I'll tell her just how much her husband loves her and how possessive he is of her.

THE AWAITER

I'D NEVER HAD ANY LUCK—MAYBE BECAUSE I NEVER thought of it, and it probably didn't think of me. Yet something was now lying at my feet. That it had wound up there was no mere accident. I could have easily stepped over it or veered to the side. Then somebody whisking about in the vicinity would have picked it up; he probably would have grinned and chalked it up to his lucky day. But I hadn't moved aside, and as long as I stood in place, glancing calmly down at it by my feet, others could only steal a wistful glimpse. Some might have regretted walking a tad too fast; if they had been slower, they could have become its possessor. Some might have reasoned, siding with themselves, that they spotted it even before I did, but they were a step too slow. Regardless, I was the one who picked up the money, without concluding as of yet whether it was my luck or not.

That evening, toward the end of monsoon season, I was walking by a crowded bus stop even though it was not on my way home and I had no purpose for taking that route. The money lay fallen behind a bus. When I bent down to pick it up, the hot air from the exhaust pipe blasted onto my face as I stood back up. A pair of eyes darted at me, whose owner walked toward me with a face painted with an uncertain smile. I knew his intentions immediately. While I myself was unsure of my status in relation to the money, one thing of which I was absolutely certain was: the man approaching was not the owner of the money—but he wanted to be.

I didn't wait for him to initiate the conversation; instead, I turned to ask a pair of university students, "Did either of you drop this?" The girls shook their heads. The man looked embarrassed and turned evasively toward the students and told them to board the bus. He turned out to be the conductor.

And the owner of the money? Where had he gone? He might be standing in that crowd without realizing that he'd dropped anything. Or he could be sitting on the bus that remained parked right there. Or he might have departed on the one before. It could also be that he happened to be passing through, like me. I clutched the money in my hand and stood hesitating for a long while. Those who found money—what did they do? People looked at me, but no one else assumed the attitude of the money's owner. They simply looked at me because I was the object of attention. I had become the most interesting thing at that moment. Those who found money, they probably tried to extract themselves as quickly as possible from the site of serendipity. But what about the owners? They probably wandered around in search. The cash that I stumbled upon, the owner dropped it only a moment ago. If I waited a little longer, he'd probably realize that his money was missing and turn around to look for it. After I returned it to him, he'd probably thank me happily. I would say to him: No need to thank me; the money remained yours all along.

I found a corner away from prying eyes and counted the sum—hundred-baht, ten-baht, and twenty-baht notes folded together: in all three hundred and eighty baht. If a person came to claim it, I should first ask how much money he'd lost, because someone might masquerade as the owner, and I would trust only the person who knew the exact amount. But what if the owner didn't know or couldn't remember how much money he had left in his pockets? I myself never kept track of the amount I carried around. But he was not I. He would probably be able to recall.

I waited . . . The bus slowly set off, the conductor looking back at me once more before disappearing into the coach. Had it been right for me to judge him? Everybody wanted to be the lucky finder of money. If I didn't have my designs on it, why didn't I step aside? The two students, too—had they spotted it, they'd probably have the same finders-keepers attitude as the conductor. Naturally, anyone would be happy to come into money. My excuse to them was, I wasn't hoping to keep the cash; I was going to wait for its owner. But if he didn't return, the money would then belong to me. But wasn't it luck? Luck was chance that could befall anyone. That it happened to me this one time was nothing strange. The conductor came here with the bus every day. The students and the other people waited for the bus daily as well. But what else could have inspired me to pass by this way, if not chance?

I felt more at ease after I came up with a worthy reason why I deserved to find the money: because I was presently awaiting its owner—the money had an owner, and surely he'd had to earn it.

It was a bunch of old bills stacked together. It might be all the money the owner had. I felt surer that he would return, even if he had no hope of recovering it, but because we humans have limited options, the choice to do something almost hopeless has to be made by those who refuse to abandon hope entirely. When he returned to discover that the money was still waiting for him, he would undoubtedly be surprised, but probably be even more thrilled.

The evening sky softened as the sun faded. One after the next, buses pulled in and funneled away; one after another, people departed with the buses. I had never had to wait for anybody this way. Maybe I had, but long ago. When I was regularly employed and led a life to which others were connected, there were people who had to wait for me, and I for them. But that was a thing of the past. I had even nearly forgotten how I once lived amid causes and consequences. And was it for that reason that we were able to endure life without feeling its emptiness? The life where one woke up each morning assured that things were waiting to be accomplished in the hours ahead? People in the city were that way: they knew the evening before when they would wake up the next day. When they got out of bed, they knew how much time they would spend on their morning routines. Once ready, they knew, too, what kind of transport to take, the color of the vehicle, where to step off. Making their way through the growing city that never kept still, a city devoid of tenderness and saturated with dog-eat-dog ambition, they had to know even more than that, to know what their paths demanded in the coming days, weeks, and months.

I was currently unemployed. This might have been one reason behind my luck. Others headed to the stop to board their bus home. The roads they pursued had a purpose. This was another reason why I deserved to find the money. I had plenty of time to wait for the owner to return for it. Out of nowhere, someone like me, someone with no aim in life like others had, wound up tasked with holding a sum of money and waiting for a person I had never met—an unfortunate individual who happened to drop his money.

I suddenly realized something else: my good fortune resulted from another's misfortune. Someone suffered bad luck in order to give someone else good luck. Must everything in the world be a zero-sum game?

In reality, I shouldn't agonize over it. There was no good or bad luck. I was waiting for the owner to come claim his money. Any moment now, all this fuss would come to an end. The owner might be realizing this very second that his money was missing—he was thinking about where he might have lost it. Give him a little time to mull it over . . . Soon the places where he might have dropped it will occur to him. He might have to retrace his steps elsewhere as well. It was conceivable he would come back here last. No matter how long it took, I would wait. I didn't have any responsibilities to attend to, no wife and children to hurry back to. It was a blessing that my life regained some semblance of purpose. For a long time now I hadn't known what I would do in the coming minutes and days. It was a welcome development for me to resume a life intertwined with others', even if ever so slightly. No matter who the owner of the money was, he was bound to be happy since he couldn't possibly imagine that his money would still be waiting for him. He'd probably feel touched by my actions. He and I might become a little bit acquainted, and if he didn't have anything pressing to do, we might walk together and chat, perhaps have a meal together. He'd probably ask me why I was still waiting, why I didn't pocket the money for myself. I already had an answer ready.

As for me, if he returned, what would I ask him? I should ask, "Why did you return? Why did you believe that your money would still be there?"

It seemed the story began and ended with the money, the sum of three hundred and eighty baht. But what was I really waiting for? I was waiting for someone, a person I believed would come back to look for his money. Why was I convinced that he would return? Was I hoping he would have faith in people's integrity, even though the whole time I'd been thinking how it was by chance that I found the money? And the owner? Would he believe in that chance? The chance that the finder of his money was not in a hurry to go anywhere and was waiting for him? The chance that the finder was more cognizant of others' misfortune than his own good luck?

The evening air didn't cool me off. On the contrary, I was simmering with anxiety. There was, in fact, no reason for me to feel that way. *He*, he who lost the money, was probably flustered and rushing back to try to recover it. But a long time had passed. I asked myself how much longer I should wait when there was no sign of anyone searching for the money.

I questioned myself anew: What was I truly waiting for? No, not merely waiting, what was I hoping for? Was it too much to expect? I was still waiting here because I believed that if I were the one to lose the money, I would return to look for it. Even I didn't find it, even if no one was waiting, I would still return. I should have some faith in the goodness of people, shouldn't I, even if it depended upon chance?

What if he didn't return? Why would he not return? Because he felt certain that he wouldn't find the money? My heart sank. Why? Why did he not place hope in people? Despite the fact that this money might have been hard-earned, that it might be the last sum for this month or until the next paycheck, that he might need it to feed his family, that a sick loved one might need it for treatment, that it might be tied to the promise to buy his children gifts, despite all this he was willing to relinquish hope and surrender to cruel destiny? Who could help tell him that I was still waiting for him? There was only he, who must tell himself—not that the money was still waiting, but that he should have faith in people . . . even if just a little.

Darkness was returning. How long could dusk last when our world was but a lightless planet? Everyone knows the evening hours must dissipate, and our world must succumb to the night. I, too . . . How much longer could I persevere in waiting for something in which one held only faint hopes, when perseverance only walks the path toward its own demise?

I continued to wonder: Why did I have to wait with perseverance? Why not wait with ease of mind? Why not wait with joy? Alas, I could only raise questions. Only reality could answer, and I couldn't twist my own feelings and turn them into something other than the response that I was persevering in my wait.

I was now confronted with another question: Why did I persist in waiting? Was it so that my hope would come to fruition? Of course I was hoping—and it was hope placed in others. Or, it wouldn't be inaccurate to say I was wishing that another person be as I imagined. Oh, what was I trying to accomplish? Did I in fact want to return the three hundred and eighty baht to its owner, or was I seeking something from that individual? Unanswered pleas to another or unfulfilled hopes in him, those were what made me endure the wait.

The bus stop was deserted. My eyes scaled the tall buildings up to the stars speckling the sky. We coexisted in close proximity on this planet. Nonetheless, we led a solitary existence; we were good or evil all alone. What right did a person have to demand something of others?

My perseverance had come to an end. And my hope in somebody else and entreaty to him had ceased as well. That moment, I was merely someone who found three hundred and eighty baht and wished to restore the money to its owner, nothing more.

I finally decided to leave the bus stop after I was able to persuade myself that the money's owner would probably not return. Only at the same time, I found that, in truth, I was still waiting.

SANDALS

TONGJAI PULLED ALL HER CLOTHES OFF THE HANGERS and threw them in a pile on the floor, leaving only her two school uniforms. She was twelve years old and finished with sixth grade; in fact, yesterday was the last time she had worn her uniform, and she was still waiting for her report card. Kui, her little brother, was sitting in the corner of the room, hunched over and crying. Tongjai had dumped his clothes on the floor in front of him, but he couldn't have cared less. From the sound of his miserable wailing, it seemed like his world was falling apart.

With the sun setting, Tongjai's white uniform shirts stood out in the darkening room. Hearing Kui's sobs, her heart grew even heavier. Although she had her clothes folded and packed in a paper bag, she couldn't find the strength to get up and light the lantern, letting the entire house become engulfed in darkness. When she heard a truck approaching, her ears perked up, and headlights poured in through the windows, casting a glow on the walls and the uniforms suspended on the rail.

Tongjai stood up and went to the window. The truck moved forward, reversed, moved forward again and then reversed again, parking with its back end in front of the gate to the chicken coop. Her father got out, followed by her mother. From the other side emerged the driver, who had a large build. The woman who owned the chicken coop walked over to them, speaking in harsh tones. The coop was completely empty, not a single chicken in sight. As her mother headed toward the house, her father grabbed a shovel and a basket, ducked down, and slipped through the doorway into the coop. Tongjai jumped up to light the lantern.

"Stop crying now, Kui. Mama's here. Pack your clothes," Tongjai commanded.

"Kids, what are you doing? Why is the house so dark?"

Tongjai came out of the room carrying the burning lamp, held its flame against another lantern's wick in the kitchen, and then returned it to the other room. Her mother unhooked the barn lantern from the crossbeam and lit it before inspecting the items that her daughter had packed in baskets. Tongjai placed the bag with her own clothes next to them, mustered every bit of courage, and waited for the right moment. But then her mother heard Kui whimpering in the other room.

"What's that noise? Is that Kui?"

"Mama, can we wait another day?" Tongjai's voice quivered.

Her mother looked at her skeptically. "Why? Why do we have to wait?"

"Kui wants to . . . he wants to go to the fair at the shrine in town." Tongjai pressed her chin down into her chest, almost panting.

Exhausted, their mother let out a soft sigh. "Oh, you want to go out and have a good time, is that it? Don't you understand why we have to leave today?"

"Yes," Tongjai said, almost in a whisper. "But if we wait until tomorrow, I'll pay the bus fare myself. I can take him."

"Oh, you're so rich! You go to school and still manage to save money while I work myself to death and still can't manage to pay off what I owe. Don't be so difficult. Go take a last look around the house. Make sure the windows are bolted. And take all this stuff out to the porch and lock up." Their mother walked over to Kui. "What are you moaning for? Or do you want the cane? Pack your clothes and go wait outside—now!" Then she marched out of the house.

Kui was sobbing even harder now, so Tongjai packed his clothes for him. She was on the verge of tears but did her best to control herself. Outside, she heard some voices yelling. Tongjai tilted her head to listen; Kui fell into a grim silence.

"Kui! Kui!" Hearing the calls, the two siblings leaped up at once and raced out to the porch. About ten children, big and small, were huddled at the bottom of the stairs. Spotting the two faces, they hollered, "Are you done yet? Let's go!" Kui sank down at the top of the stairs, his cheeks stained with tears. Tongjai went back inside to grab the barn lantern and carried it out to the porch. She sat down, clutching the railing as she observed the cheery faces below.

"I can't go anymore," Kui told them. "My mama said no."

The other children urged him to sneak out, saying that even though he would get the cane when he came home, the pain would be over the next day. Kui scooted down two steps, but Tongjai stopped him before he got any farther. As his friends took off, he leaned his face against the railing and burst into tears. One of the older boys, about Tongjai's age, hung back. He got off his bike, walked closer, and looked up at the porch.

"How come?" Gaew asked.

"We've got to help our parents work tomorrow—a job harvesting sugarcane," Tongjai responded. "A truck came to buy fertilizers for the farm next door, so Mama's having us hitch a ride with them tonight. We're going any minute now."

The boy looked crestfallen. "When are you coming back? Have you told your mom about the new school?"

Her eyes red and nose dripping, Tongjai tried as best she could to keep her feelings inside, but her voice betrayed her.

"I don't know how long the job will take. At least several days . . . maybe a few weeks. And my mama said I won't be going to school anymore. We don't have the money."

"But didn't you tell her that they're treating you as a special case, how you don't have to take the entrance exam to get in? If you don't go to this school, you won't get to play music anymore. Did you already tell her that?"

"Yeah, I told her."

"Did you tell her that you're going to be the *jakae* soloist? She doesn't know about that, does she?"

"She knows. She knows everything. But we don't have the money."

Gaew's head dropped; he felt defeated. He had been longing to play with Tongjai again. The year before, when he was in sixth grade and Tongjai in fifth, they got to see each other every time the band practiced. At the solo competition, they had both come back with awards. After sixth grade, he moved on to the new school. They had exempted him from the entrance exam because of his musical talent, and he had been nicely paving the way for Tongjai. She had promised to apply to the same school, so they could once again play in the same band. She had promised they would go together . . . no matter where. Gaew looked up at her. Her head was bowed, completely still. Where her right cheek was visible under the glow of the lantern, silent tears were flowing down.

"But . . ." Tongjai met his eyes. "If we make enough money from this job, maybe Mama will let me keep going to school. I'll ask her again when we come back."

Gaew's eyes glimmered slightly. "Don't forget. Beg until she says yes. And do you have to leave now? You should stay so we can go to the fair together, at least for one night."

"We're off as soon as my mama and papa are done loading the chicken manure onto the truck. You go ahead."

Tongjai went back in the house, bolted all the windows, checked their belongings, and then carried the baskets outside. After extinguishing all the lanterns and locking up, she sat there waiting in the dark. Gaew was gone.

The chicken manure on the truck gave off a vicious stench. Kui fought as hard as he could, kicking and screaming. Their mother tried to get him to sit up front, but he threw such a tantrum that she got mad. He said he hated her and didn't want to sit with her. Their father said fine, if he was going to be that way, he could sit in the back, and he laid a tarp over the mound of manure for Kui to sit on. Nervously, Tong-jai asked if she could ride with her brother. As they set off, she spotted Gaew riding his bike out of a shadow, closely following the truck. She could make out his face, but then the truck accelerated, leaving him farther and farther behind. Soon Gaew disappeared into the darkness.

The stink lessened with the quickening breeze. The truck drove past stretches of rice paddies as it made its way out of their village. When the fair came into view, Tongjai told Kui to look. He sat up, his eyes wide. Over there, lights shone bright, and the thumping of the music drifted over, together with the sounds of the MC's banter and a slew of other things. A white movie screen loomed over the fair grounds. The film hadn't started yet, but soon a picture appeared on the screen.

"The sandals ad!" Kui blurted out. Tongjai knew it, too.

A woman walked over to another woman, who was sitting down. Almost in time with the first, Kui recited her line, "You want to go to the market?" The seated woman replied, together with Tongjai, "Okay." In front of the door was an array of flip-flops. The two women each put on a pair and walked off. The picture cut to another woman lounging on a beach chair. She was wearing what looked to them like a skimpy floral set of bra and panties, her breasts and buttocks spilling out, luring the viewers' eyes. A man in his underwear, or so it appeared, walked over and stood in front of her. "Do you want to take a walk?" Kui and the man asked at the same time. "Sure," Tongjai responded along with the woman. The pair put on their flip-flops and strolled along the beach holding hands, her porcelain butt cheeks showing. The screen was soon obstructed by trees, and they grew denser and denser along the road until nothing more could be seen.

The two children looked at each other, giggling. Although Kui didn't realize it, his tears had dried, but Tongjai was laughing so hard her eyes were watering. The siblings tried to recall what happened next in the commercial. Tongjai thought the same woman would be standing on the beach, with flip-flops arranged in a circle nearby. She had seen the clip twice, but Kui, who had seen it only once, argued that, no, the woman would be standing by the pool. And in fact, he was correct: the camera would pan down from the woman's face to the whiskey glass that she held in front of her cleavage, then to her belly button, her tiny bathing suit and her legs, finally pausing at the flip-flops on her feet. By the side of the pool, sandals would be arranged in a circle.

But then Kui remembered his predicament. He wasn't getting to go to the fair at the shrine like the other kids. He thought about the Chinese opera theater, the *likay* stage, the Ferris wheel, the merry-go-round, the shooting games, the cotton candy, the balloons. Why did his mother have to be meaner than everyone else's? All the kids from the neighborhood were probably headed to the Zeng Tek Xiang Tung Shrine, hanging in their own cliques, passing other groups of kids from their and other neighborhoods as they roamed around. Each and every thing was sure to dazzle and excite. Toys and treats would be on offer all over the grounds. The shrine held its fair once a year, for three days. Kui got to go for the first time only last year, and only on the last night. This year he would miss all three nights. If only his mother were a little nicer and let him go just for tonight—they could have left for work tomorrow. He hated his mother, intensely hated her. He couldn't believe he wasn't getting to go to the fair this year. But he was still hoping for a miracle. He prayed that the truck would break down, and prayed that one of his parents would get such a bad stomachache that they would have to turn around and go back.

"What's wrong, Kui? We were laughing just now." Tongjai stared at him, but it was too dark for her to be able to make out his face.

"I hate Mama!" he yelled. "Because of her, I'm the unluckiest kid on earth. I wish I'd been born someone else!"

Tongjai sighed, expelling the horrible stench that she had just inhaled. Kui's words made her think: *should have been born someone else*. She really wondered, if she weren't Tongjai, what would her life be like? What would she be doing now? She could be Supa, the richest kid in her class. Then she'd probably be lazing around in that beautiful house. But Supa was such an awful student. She failed two or three subjects every exam period. Still, Supa got fifty baht of allowance for school every day, and the treats and fruit she brought always looked delicious. She had pretty stationery with unusual designs that no one else had. Things that she got tired of, she simply gave away to her classmates. What a charmed life! Tongjai wanted to try being Supa for a day or two; it couldn't be so bad. Let Supa come and ride in this truck full of chicken crap with Kui. Let her get up early tomorrow morning, eat rice with salt-cured fish, and go work as a farmhand harvesting sugarcane. That was as far as Tong-jai got, but the idea made her laugh. Kui looked at her, confused.

"Kui, if you don't want to be yourself, who do you want to be? Have you ever thought about it?"

"I don't want to be anybody."

"I want to try trading places with Supa. Do you remember her? Supa, my friend with the peacock at home? I can be her and she'll have to go cut sugarcane instead. If you don't trade with anyone, then you have to go cut sugarcane with Supa. Me, in a minute, I'm going to go buy myself a pretty pair of shoes."

"You're talking crazy," Kui snapped, his anger still raging. "I'm not going. Just watch. I'm praying for Mama and Papa to get stomachaches, both of them."

Tongjai had had it with him. "Enough. You're taking this too far, Kui. You need to learn to put up with things, to have some patience. They have the fair every year. You can wait and go next time. Stop whining and tell yourself that you're going to wait and go next year."

"I'm not going to wait. You just watch."

"So what are you going to do then? You're not going to get to go. I told you, you have to tell yourself to wait. If you can do that, then you won't be upset about it. The fair isn't so important. If you try being me, you'd know. From now on I'll never get to do anything. I won't get to go to school. I won't get to see my friends, my teachers. I won't get to play music. All day every day, I'll be out working as a farmhand, like Mama and Papa have done for over ten years. I don't have a single thing to hope for, and still I'm ... I'm waiting for the right opportunity, the right moment. Maybe Mama will change her mind and let me go back to school. No matter how long it takes, I can wait. You have to be able to wait, too."

Kui said nothing in response; he simply dragged his forearm across his face, wiping away his tears. Then he moved toward the side of the truck and pulled himself up, grabbing onto the edge. Tongjai told him to sit back down, but he acted as if he didn't hear. Making his way to the back, he looked like he was about to jump out. Tongjai panicked, cried for him to stop, but it was too late. She screamed, telling her mother to stop the truck, but no one heard her. Kui's body lying on the road was about to be swallowed up by darkness.

Tongjai couldn't wait any longer. She wasn't going to get a better chance. She didn't even have a second to pause and contemplate. She dived after him. In that moment, she was dreaming of the beach, the breaking waves, and she imagined her body was a sandal, floating adrift in the middle of the ocean.

KANDA'S EYEBROWS

MY WIFE HAS NO EYEBROWS. WHAT SHE HAS INSTEAD are black tattoos mimicking their arched shapes. When she was younger, she didn't use to look like this. Now her jaws seem wider, her cheeks have started to sag, and she has become thicker, on top and bottom. I wonder if anyone remembers how my wife, in her youth, was the most beautiful woman around.

I find it unnerving how fast women's looks change. This is something I've been preoccupied with since I was young. I have noted, as I observed more women, that there are some exceptions to the rule. These female outliers were what I'd always dreamed of finding. For most women, family life seems to weigh them down with obligations that men often can't imagine. The burden falls on their fragile shoulders and pins them down until they become conditioned and surrender themselves to their new role, forsaking their beauty and losing the fire that makes them want to show off or flirt around their husbands.

When pursuing women they desire, young men, consumed by lust, are infatuated with every inch of their girlfriends. And the ladies, even the ugly ones, are all eager to flaunt themselves for their lovers. Their beauty shines brightest during this period. But once they settle down, the husbands are caught off guard by their wives' transformation. Every part of youthful female beauty, once so affecting, slowly begins to fade. Before five years of married life have passed, the husband is living with another person, someone completely different. Because of this, I respect women who make the effort to primp for their husbands for as long as possible.

My wife used to be stunning. When we first saw Kanda, the five of us—my four friends and I—all vied for her attention. Because she didn't readily show interest in any of us, she appeared to be even more beautiful and more complex. She smiled at all of us; she was equally friendly with each of us, which made us even more determined. My friends and I worked at a car dealership. When we spotted Kanda for the first time, she was walking past the dealership's showroom, dressed to the nines, making her way to the crosswalk down the block. She worked at the little real estate agency across the street.

With the five of us, it was always the same old story: whenever a woman entered the fray, Wonchai, that handsome bastard, was chosen every time. We were all pretty fed up. We thought badly of those women, questioning their taste. In every way, aside from his good looks, Wonchai was clearly the inferior man. He had a playboy's roving eye and the body language to match, and his flirtatious way of engaging in conversation didn't exactly inspire trust. Still, we had to concede that most women were into men like him. Kanda was the first girl to look coolly past Wonchai's attractiveness. We were beside ourselves—the woman of our dreams had finally materialized.

Every week we invited Kanda out with us, to catch a movie, go work out, have a picnic. Without fail, it was Kanda and the five of us. This woman was unbelievable. She didn't put on airs, wasn't easily upset, wasn't fussy. She was cheerful, smart, and honest. We made a pact among ourselves: if she fell in love with one of us, that lucky guy would make her his wife and be a faithful husband to her, and no matter whom she chose, the rest of us would be happy for him.

But Kanda's eventual pick upset us. No way in the world, no one could believe she went for the bastard Wonchai. It transpired one night at a beachside hotel when the lover boy snuck into her room. In the morning we demanded an explanation. Wonchai insisted that he hadn't forced her, that Kanda had feelings for him and was all too willing. We didn't believe him. Kanda herself was tight-lipped. In the days that followed, circumstances changed, and we backed off. Kanda openly became Wonchai's girlfriend. I don't know what the others thought—certainly we all wished things had turned out differently—but me, I was thinking further ahead: she was in for a struggle. Even though Wonchai, too, had sworn that he would marry Kanda and be faithful, we all knew his words were meaningless. In predicting this, I felt like I was counting down the days until Kanda's inevitable heartbreak.

Still, I had to admit, albeit grudgingly, that a beautiful young couple was greater than the sum of their parts. Kanda and Wonchai enhanced one another, each looking even better than before. Outside of our group of friends, who knew too much about Wonchai's character, people all lavished praise on the pair. Whenever I heard these compliments, I fled to my group of friends. I grumbled to them about how the others didn't have a clue and how their remarks were so irritating. Oh, how superficial appearance is, and how superficial these people's opinions.

That damned gorgeous couple lasted longer than expected. But the honeymoon period eventually came to an end. Even though Wonchai claimed he would marry Kanda, he kept drumming up excuses to postpone the engagement. We began to suspect that he was falling for someone new. The little changes weren't hard to notice. He often disappeared, he was cagey, but his face had a glow about it, and he was uncharacteristically upbeat. Kanda started being unable to locate her boyfriend, and my friends and I had to cover up for his absences. No, I didn't do it to help a friend, not at all. I did it for her sake, to keep her happy, as I didn't want to see her down; I did it for the sake of her steadfast heart, which had never harbored any misgivings about her lover. But ultimately, I did it for the sake of her luminous beauty, which only increased with each passing day.

All of that faded into the background as we grew apart, but later on my friends and I took renewed interest in Kanda's well-being. This time was different, however; the impulse behind our concern for her was humanitarian. I wished her well and pitied her deeply. We protected her as if she were a delicate flower. In fact, by that time my three friends all had girlfriends poised to be their future wives. I was the only one who had never had a steady relationship. Because Kanda had won us over, we swooped in to protect her like brothers looking out for their little sister.

We cornered Wonchai for a series of interrogations. Each time he swore that Kanda was the woman he was going to marry. As for the other girls, they were just little pleasures. When urged to quit womanizing, he was visibly annoyed that his friends were overstepping their bounds. We had no choice but to back off. And so we continued to conceal it from Kanda.

True, we were all worried about her, but the others could only spare so much time since they had girlfriends. I was the only single one left. As a result, I was more upset by Kanda's predicament than the rest. It bothered me so much that I decided to try to expose Wonchai, even though we had spent years covering up for him. I didn't tell anyone about my plan because I knew my friends wouldn't approve. The opportunity presented itself one day when I successfully split away, covertly waited for Kanda at her workplace, and took her to dinner alone.

Walking side by side with her into the restaurant—I'll never forget that moment. I still get worked up just thinking about it. In that instant I was giddy, wondering what it would be like if we, these two people now walking next to each other, were in love. It would be pure bliss, and everything would fall into place. Kanda would no longer be taken advantage of by a guy whose only redeeming quality was his looks. I liked how the waitstaff peered at us. I liked how the other diners turned to look at us and then whispered. I wanted the whole world to get an eyeful of us together.

Kanda was truly beautiful. Like I said, she was the kind of woman I had always dreamed of. Being with that handsome bastard for three years hadn't tarnished her beauty one bit. Strangely, she was exponentially more beautiful. Because of her loveliness, when we sat facing each other, I was speechless. I suddenly realized: If finding out about Wonchai's infidelities caused her to suffer, would the sadness or distress affect her beauty? According to my observations, that tended to be the case with women. The more I considered the idea, the more flustered I became. I could only stare at Kanda's face, awestruck by her beauty. Then the answer dawned on me. Kanda wasn't like other girls. She had proven time and time again that she was different. So I became convinced that her beauty played by different rules. Nothing in the world could fracture or destroy it. Even with the passing of time, her beauty would merely adapt to her age. Therefore, I made a decision.

After preparing her for the blow, prompting her to steady herself and stay strong, I divulged to her in detail Wonchai's skirt-chasing ways, his trysts, and his putting off their marriage. When I finished, I waited for her reaction. But, nothing. She was unmoved and silent, as if she had been listening to a story about someone else entirely. I was the one who got worked up, worried she didn't believe me.

Kanda smiled graciously. She said softly, measuring her words, that she had known for a long time what I had just told her. In fact, she knew even more than what I had reported, and she didn't see it as a problem. I was dumbstruck. Her thinking was beyond comprehension. Not only that, she said she had already prepared herself for this sort of thing—that women tend to have methods at their disposal that men couldn't imagine. Indeed, it was beyond my imagination and comprehension. The outcome of our conversation depressed me. A beloved man's betrayal was no longer a problem nowadays? And she even bragged about having a method for dealing with it. Was she being smart or profoundly stupid? Or was the willingness to be stupid part of her plan? What was it all for? To keep a worthless man? Huh. I still didn't want to believe that a beautiful woman like Kanda could fall prey to a man like Wonchai that she would submit her body and soul to him.

"I don't agree with you at all," I told her, letting my tone and facial expression say the same. I asked, Didn't she know she was beautiful? Her beauty should be pursued and respected. Men should submit to her because of it. Kanda cracked up as she listened. I grew red-faced with anger. Too furious to hold my words back, I told her to stop laughing. I told her, since we'd gotten to know her, my friends and I had all come to deeply care for her and truly had her interests at heart. Our discovery that our friend was doing her wrong only made us more concerned. We constantly thought about how we could help. But the fact that she was utterly unperturbed made a mockery of our goodwill.

My words had an immediate effect. Kanda was stunned, her pretty face visibly saddened. A moment later, she uttered the appropriate line, "And what should I do?" Able to smile then, I started to comfort her.

Because she had been loyal all along, she was entitled to feel self-righteous. She shouldn't look the other way and be willing to tolerate a punishment not of her own making. Because of this, and the hints I'd been dropping, each time Wonchai disappeared without an explanation after that, Kanda tracked him down and dragged him back. The couple fought more and more viciously, and within a few months, they were history.

I was the only one left to take Kanda out afterward to help her lick her wounds. One night at a hotel by the beach, I invited myself into her room. She fully acquiesced. I was in a paradise like no other that night.

That was ten years ago. Now let me explain how she has been, and how I have been, since we got married.

Just a few days after our wedding, I woke up in the morning and rolled over toward her, intending to wake her up by planting a kiss on her eyelid. But I was stopped in my tracks—I stared, petrified, at her eyebrows. They were so peculiar: the thin little black arches contained not a single eyebrow hair. Astonished, I ogled for a long while: How long had they been this way? Why hadn't I noticed? I inspected the other parts of her face—eyes, nose, mouth—and I was relieved that nothing else was out of order. Without makeup, her face was washed out, drawing attention to the hairless, coal-black eyebrows. Growing more and more distressed, I slowly moved away from her and laid my head on the pillow, trying to console myself, trying to make myself stop focusing on such a trivial matter. Still, I couldn't help but glance at the protrusive black eyebrows again and again.

Frankly, I'd never trusted Kanda from the start. Her beauty could catch the interest of other men, and I didn't want to have any problems in our marriage. She quit her job without a fight; her professional life came to an end and she became a homemaker. Our relationship was fine, but I came to realize that it had been a mistake to have Kanda quit working. Since she didn't have to leave the house, she practically never applied makeup anymore. I got to see her dressed up only occasionally, when we went out. But matters became worse the more she got used to not wearing makeup. It tormented me. All you could see on her face were the hovering black eyebrows. Even after I'd had several months to grow accustomed to them, I just couldn't let it go. When we talked, I didn't dare look her in the eye—I couldn't control myself: whenever I looked at her face, my damn eyes went straight to her eyebrows.

People tend to get what they fear most. My beautiful Kanda had vanished. I was living with a stranger, an unfamiliar face: a woman who made no effort to take care of herself, who ran herself ragged with housework, who was always sweaty, her face oily. Her hair was haphazardly pulled back and clipped to the middle of her head with something or other. It was like that every day. Oh, how unfair it was. Oh, Kanda! I'd loved her since the first time I'd laid eyes on her, loved her unfailingly, loved her tenderly. Even though I wasn't the first man in her life, I never quibbled. When I finally snagged her, it was as though I'd been cheated. I'd obviously been cheated!

After keeping it bottled up for two years, I decided to say something. We were watching TV. I had been preparing for the encounter since early evening, but nothing came out of my mouth until after ten p.m. Unsure whether what I was going to demand from Kanda was my due right or something overblown that might be the object of her scorn and ridicule, I began to doubt myself. Because of this, I swapped my tough stance for a tease. A comedy was on. I chose a moment when she was laughing loudly to suddenly crane over and stare at her face, assuming a puzzled expression. "Hmm, why are your eyebrows like that?" I exclaimed, as if I had never seen the eyebrow-shaped tattoos before. I was hoping she'd be embarrassed in response, so I readied myself to comfort her, to counsel her that the tattoos wouldn't look so bad if she only made herself up prettily like she used to. But the next second, Kanda, trying to stifle a laugh, replied, "What? Did you really just notice? They've been like that for ages!" I laughed softly, to show that I didn't think too much of the matter. We continued to watch the movie. Even though I was losing hope, I brought up the eyebrows again, keeping my tone as light as possible: "But why are they like that? And since when?" The movie had hit an uninteresting stretch, so Kanda related in full how she had gone and had a doctor permanently remove her eyebrow hairs and put tattoos in their place. This had happened three years before she met my friends and me. I listened with my eyes fixed on the TV. Eventually, I feigned laughter, supposedly at something on screen, but it was really to make her stop talking. I was so humiliated that she had no shame about her lack of eyebrow hairs.

That was eight years ago. I endured the situation for another three years. Then we got into a massive fight, and I think I must have brutally criticized her about how she was letting herself go.

What happened was, we were going to a friend's wedding, and I had gotten this idea into my head that if I took her to a party where people were going to be dressed to impress, she wouldn't let herself be upstaged. As I was waiting for her to get ready, I reminisced about the day she and I had stepped into that restaurant together, how everyone had been staring at us. I wanted the old Kanda back; I wanted to have the marvelous Kanda on my arm and parade past the other wedding guests, who would all have their eyes on us. But when Kanda came out of the room, my dreams were shattered. She was dressed like my mother! Her face was powdered but not made-up, and her jet-black eyebrows were bolder than ever. I had meticulously tucked in my shirt, but as soon as I saw her, I stood up and yanked the tails out from under my waistband.

During our fight, I even brought up Wonchai. I was furious and used some strong language, saying that she was a woman with no brain, infatuated with a man who had nothing going for him but his looks, that not even his womanizing bothered her. Even though she knew she'd been betrayed, she still wanted to make herself look more and more beautiful for him. Me, the man who was faithful to her and only her, she repaid me by looking increasingly shabby. Why was that? At first Kanda just stared at me, bewildered. When she realized that I had a problem with her appearance, *then* she blew up. She lectured me like I was a child, saying how foolish I was to fixate on looks. I lashed back, arguing that no, she didn't get it, I wasn't making the demand because I was a fool, but because of how well I knew her. I knew her better than anyone else in the world because no one else observed her, noticed things about her, and watched her every move. She was the sort of woman who cared about beauty, so much so that during all those years my friends and I were constantly spending time with her, no one ever saw her face without makeup. But she changed after we got married. Why was that? "Why? Why? Why?" I screamed in her face, badgering her for an answer.

Nodding her head in quick succession, Kanda looked like she had an answer ready. She glared at me silently for some time, and then sighed. In the end, all I could do was keep my mouth shut.

We both dropped the subject and never mentioned it again. That was five years ago. These days I don't know whether or not she's let it go. Last night was the first time in ten years that I had to sleep alone because Kanda was away visiting relatives in the provinces. Maybe because I wasn't used to it, or who knows why, but I couldn't sleep all night. My damn mind kept dredging up old problems, making them return to haunt me. Close to dawn, exhausted from trying to chase away my own thoughts, I settled on one line of inquiry: the expression on Kanda's face five years ago. What was it that she was going to say but didn't? What were the words that were on the tip of her tongue that night? I clung tightly to this question as I waited for her to return.

It's three in the afternoon on Sunday. As I wait for Kanda to arrive, I'm resolute, as focused as someone meditating. A quarter past, she lugs her things into the house, giving me a withered smile. She sets her stuff down and gets some water from the refrigerator. I sit quietly, sternly following her with my gaze. She notices my silence as she puts her glass down. Yes, it's time.

"Kanda, have a seat. There's something I want to talk to you about."

She sits down, looking alarmed.

"Do you remember that time we fought, five years ago?" She nods. "The time we were going to somebody's wedding and you looked so frumpy, I couldn't stand it, so we had a huge blowout fight?"

"I remember. Why?"

"Yeah, that time. We argued, and I said, you're the kind of person who cares about her appearance, and then after you married me, you changed. With other women, it might be par for the course, but with you I don't buy it. To me, it's clearly a calculated move on your part. Why is that, Kanda? I asked you this five years ago, and you were about to answer, and then you changed your mind. Now tell me. What was it you meant to say that day?"

Kanda closes her eyes, letting out a deep sigh, and then sinks back in her chair.

"Listen, Kanda. We're not going to fight like we did that time. I just want to know the answer, and that will be the end of it. This is the last time."

"Gleur, I just don't understand how you're still hung up on this. The fact that we've been together just fine until now already proves that this isn't important." She sighs again. "What does it matter whether I was pretty or not before? I'm thirty-eight, and you're forty. We're already old! Why don't you worry about other things, like buying a plot of land for a house, or why we still don't have children?"

"Why are you bringing up other things? I just want an answer, and that's it. I promise. Once you answer me, I'll end this discussion immediately."

"What if you're so upset by my answer that you won't end the discussion?"

Hit with those words, I feel my face and body flush. There, she let it slip. The all-important reason *does* exist. "What is it, Kanda? Tell me what it is."

She sighs deeply. "No, I can't. I shouldn't."

"Tell me, Kanda." I start to raise my voice. "Why is

it that with me you let yourself go and wear those awful clothes? And why is it that with Wonchai you always managed to look good? Tell me now. You've already tortured me for ten years!"

"Why do you have to bring Wonchai into this? He's got nothing to do with it."

"Nothing? Then you should be able to tell me why you always looked so beautiful when you were with him. Don't think I don't notice the difference. You looked your best back then, despite how terribly he treated you, starting from the moment that he . . . he . . . forced himself on you. Once he had you locked down as his girlfriend, he got tired of you in no time and left you for someone else. In that situation, you looked more beautiful than ever. But with me—"

"What are you saying, Gleur? You're painting quite a picture. Who forced himself on me? Nobody ever said it was anything but consensual. Why are you still deluding yourself?"

"What about the fact that he left you for other women?"

"Actually, he didn't leave me. He was a womanizer; I already knew that about him. The fact that he'd have something on the side was to be expected. The real reason we broke up was . . . was you."

I feel my heart jerk, like a fish being pounded on the head. Listen—listen to what she's saying. I helped her all this time, only to be stung by her words. The way she's talking, anybody who hears her would think the same. "You still have feelings for him, don't you, Kanda?" I said. "Oh, Kanda, you really had me fooled. I thought you were different from other women, but you're just one of those pretty faces with nothing behind it. You and that empty shell of a man deserve each other. Then why are you with me, Kanda?"

"Ugh!" Kanda jumps up and puts her hands on her waist. "You've completely forgotten why I ended up with you, haven't you? It's because *you* forced yourself on me. I didn't want to, and you knew it. I stayed with you because I thought, at least you truly loved me, even though . . . even though . . . Huh!" Kanda plops herself down hard on the chair, clutching her head in her hands.

I'm numb in my seat, looking at her in shock. "What is it, Kanda? Even though what? What were you going to say? Say it!" I yell, losing all restraint.

Kanda lets go of her head and slowly looks up at me. "You really want to know?" Her voice is ice-cold. "Fine." She stands up and walks toward the bathroom. When I see her taking the mirror down off the wall, I feel a sharp, stabbing pain in my chest. I'm terrified. I want to run away, but it's too late. Kanda holds the mirror in front of me, and a face appears. Oh, no, no, no. I shake my head, tears running down my face. No, please no. I don't want to see my face. Kanda holds the mirror right in front of me, even as I'm trying to fend her off.

"Have a good look. It's that. It's because of that grotesquely hideous face of yours that I had to stop looking so good. Do you have any idea how embarrassing it is to go out together and have everyone stare at us? Do you think I don't know how disgusting my eyebrows look without makeup? But it beats looking pretty and then having to walk side by side with a man with that face." Kanda violently jabs the mirror with her finger.

I start sobbing hysterically, beating my chest and slapping my face. Kanda goes to put the mirror back. She doesn't even try to comfort me. I run into the bedroom, rip the sheet off, and knot it at one end. Then I come out again, toss the sheet over the door, and clamp it shut above the knot. All the while, I'm groaning, "I'm not going to live anymore. I don't want to live anymore. I'd rather die!" I make a loop, stuff my head through it, and fold my legs, letting my weight fall so the noose tightens around my neck. Kanda walks into the kitchen without even so much as a glance in my direction. I make choking noises to get her attention, but there is no sign of her coming to my side. I can't breathe so I stand up and take the sheet off my neck. Rushing into the kitchen, I see Kanda serving herself dinner. I grab a knife, turn my back to her, and pretend to plunge it into my stomach repeatedly. "I don't want to be on this earth anymore!" I moan.

Slamming the pot down, Kanda leaves without a word. I put the knife down and chase after her. She's on her way out. I catch a glimpse of her back. She's heading into the house next door. She's going to play cards. Kanda always plays cards when something's bothering her.

I limp back into the house, drop down on the bed, and cry.

THE DOCTOR

THE DOCTOR MOVED BACK SEVERAL DAYS AFTER THE start of monsoon season. The sun blistered intensely in the morning hours, and in the afternoons, a lazy breeze would come, followed by rain clouds rolling in from the east, drawing a canopy high up in the sky. The clouds hovered lower in the evenings, turning a deep gray, signaling rain. Sometimes when dark clouds embraced the sky in the east and the horizon to the west was clear, the sun would make an appearance late in the day, casting its golden light on the uneven dirt roads, which were full of potholes and puddles. Trees stood bathing in the yellow sun, their bright green leaves springing out in stark contrast to the stormy sky.

The doctor was no stranger. He had lived in the village for almost ten years before something had caused him to move away. At the moment, the road was slippery with mud. The kids had all caught colds and were dripping at the nose. Even the adults were sneezing and coughing hard, and could be seen one after another with their necks bent forward, hacking up phlegm. No one was yet aware of the doctor's return, aside from his landlady. He had planned to arrive late at night in order to avoid running into people. Perhaps it wasn't so much that he didn't want to see the folks he used to know, but more that he feared they might pretend not to recognize him. The night of his arrival, if the neighbors had been jolted awake by the sound of the metal gate opening and happened to be curious enough, if half-asleep, to get up and inspect, they would see two men moving boxes and furniture. At first the observers might take them for burglars, the way they were tiptoeing around like they didn't want to make a sound. But once more awake, those watching would be able to accurately process the scene: the belongings that the men were endeavoring to move weren't being carried from the house to the truck but from the truck into the house. Once they were finished, one of the men handed money to the other, who took it and left.

The doctor stood by the side of the truck for a while longer, shifting his weight as he took in the surrounding homes and the treetops and the lights along the eaves of the shophouses, which illuminated their metal gates, all tightly shut. He looked at his wristwatch: it was past two in the morning. The doctor amused himself with the thought that someone could be secretly watching him at that moment, realizing the old doctor had returned. As the idea crossed his mind, he sensed a pair of eyes spying on him. He stood still, peering into an open window on the second floor of one of the shophouses. But as hard as he stared, he saw nothing but darkness. He quickly locked the truck, went inside the house, shut his front gate, and, after arranging himself a place to sleep, went to bed with excitement in his heart.

The next morning, as soon as he noticed daylight starting to creep in, he got up. He heard clacking noises outside his front gate and the indistinct sound of conversation. Word of his return had spread, it seemed. The doctor felt somewhat relieved. But when he thought about how the situation was going to play out, his momentary relief fled him, and he sighed heavily. He eyed his belongings, still in piles all over the place. He needed to spend the whole day organizing.

After he showered and dressed, the doctor thought of the *kwaychap*-noodle shop next to the grocery across the street. He pictured the faces of the many people he'd recognize along the way. Craving a hot bowl of *kwaychap*, he tried to come up with the right words to greet them. But after thinking about it for a while, he lost his appetite and dug out the electric kettle to boil some water. He made coffee and ate some stale bread.

The doctor stayed shut up inside the house and didn't open the front gate until evening. Throughout the entire day, his thoughts and actions were rather misaligned. He worked up a sweat and wore himself out, straining to move a large table by running back and forth, pushing one side and then the other. After the table came the bed and the wardrobe, which he moved in a similar manner. It took him a long time to get everything in place. But he wasn't exactly focused: the sound of the table legs dragging on the floor might have grated on the ears of passersby, but it sent him into a deep reverie. He thought of the villagers, the people who had once been his patients. During the two years he'd been away, where had they gone to seek treatment? Unless a case was severe enough to warrant a hospital, the local public health center was too far. With those thoughts going through his mind, the doctor kept losing track of what he was doing, and he made his furniture appear confused and aimless: when a piece looked like it wanted to move toward the left, it would somehow wind up to the right; or when it seemed to be gliding forward, it would end up going backward.

The doctor felt himself getting tense. Now that he'd returned, he couldn't decide if he should behave like a doctor or like any other villager. And how should he arrange his furniture—like a home or like a clinic? He decided to arrange it as if it were an ordinary home, no matter how much he wanted it to be a clinic, because the villagers might not ultimately accept him as their doctor, might not want to be the patients of a fake doctor like him. He converted his old consultation desk into a reading desk: in lieu of bottles of medications and various apparatuses, he piled large stacks of books on top. He angled his low glass cabinet so that its wooden back was facing the door, and pushed his desk up against it; the cabinet's shelves were still stuffed with medicine bottles large and small. He put up a screen, behind which had once been a hospital cot; he now used this space as his bedroom, making the cot his own bed by removing the white pillowcase and sheets and storing them, to be replaced with matching patterned bedding that he had unpacked. He pushed the bed against the wall, hammered a nail above it, and hooked a hanger there. He then tested out his new bed. It was high and narrow, but that was all right; he could sleep there. His old bedroom he converted into a storage room, the other bed now a surface on which to pile things.

Once everything had found its place, the doctor started to clean: sweep, wipe, mop. It started drizzling outside, and the dreary atmosphere instantly dragged down his spirits. He moved about the house listlessly, longing for the old days, wishing for everything to return to the way it had once been. In a person's lifetime, ten years weren't insignificant. He had dedicated everything to the villagers when he was their doctor. Was there anybody who hadn't been cared for and attended to by him? People had recovered with his remedies, with his advice, which had all proven effective. No matter what it was that had helped them heal, he had never questioned his own status as a doctor. It might have been illegal, he might not have been licensed, but deep in his bones and in his soul, he was a doctor, and the only acknowledgment he needed was from himself and his patients. The bond between them ran deeper than the typical doctor-patient relationship. He loved these people, and they loved and respected him back—at least they used to.

He finished his tasks just as it became dark enough to switch on the lights. After starting the rice, he went to go take a shower. Once dressed, he went through a long deliberation before deciding to open the gate, folding each side as far apart from the other as it would go. He went to stand under the porch light, his eyes doing a broad sweep of the street. Several people walking down the road turned to look at him—he couldn't decipher their expressions—and then they quickly averted their eyes and carried on as before. But, observing closer, he could practically smell the forced nonchalance of the passersby, not stopping to say hello, not giving him a smile, and some even staying all the way on the other side of the road. Auntie Yong's grocery, which was slightly kitty-corner from him, had turned its bright lights on, illuminating all the goods that were jammed in there. The doctor didn't see Auntie Yong, who could usually be found sitting in front of the shop. He spotted only her daughter and her grandchild, who were in the middle of transacting with a customer. He considered going to buy canned fish and some other supplies, but he still felt hesitant. Five doors down to the left of the grocery was Dang's barbershop. There were four or five young men hanging out in there chatting, but he didn't see Dang. Eventually, the doctor went back inside and sat at his desk, sulking with his chin in his hands, looking rather like he could be waiting for patients.

A man of a certain age, neatly dressed with his shirt tucked in, brought himself to a stop in front of the house. Without waiting for the doctor's invitation, he removed his shoes and confidently stepped inside. He pulled a chair back and plunked himself down. The doctor suddenly assumed a professional air, putting on an inquisitive face and lowering his hands away from his chin and onto the table.

The man looked left and right and then down at the ground. "Your clinic looks a bit odd," he remarked eventually. "I came here to get some IV fluids administered, maybe a bottle—but it looks strange here."

The doctor swallowed. "You'd like IV fluids? Who recommended you?"

"People in the village said you'd come back, doctor. At first I thought I'd go to the public health station, but then I thought here would be better. I live just one street over—you probably don't know me. I moved here after you left," the man said as he looked around.

"There's nothing strange about how this place looks.

It's just that, this isn't actually a clinic, and you don't have to call me 'doctor' because I'm not, in fact, a doctor."

"I see . . . the matter with you not being a doctor, I've already heard about it, but people say you're still able to treat patients and you don't charge a lot. The only thing is, this clinic doesn't look much like a clinic in my opinion."

The doctor became tongue-tied. He was so interested in what the man was saying that his cheeks twitched. Once he managed to pull himself together, he quickly asked, "What else have you heard? What have the villagers said about me? Can you tell me?"

The man tightened his lips into a grin, pitying the doctor's apparent eagerness. "You come up in conversation just about every day. So this isn't a clinic anymore then? That's too bad. I was thinking I could come here for a bottle of IV fluids. I just got over a fever, but I still feel tired and a bit weak."

"Oh . . . well, let me explain. If it's really necessary, this could still be a clinic." Once the words had left his mouth, the doctor felt like flinging his arms wide open, welcoming the old days back with a warm embrace. He couldn't believe the villagers didn't mind that he wasn't a "real" doctor. They didn't think that he'd fooled them; their reaction was nothing like what he'd been so afraid of this whole time. He leaped to his feet and gestured toward the screen, saying, "You can go ahead and wait on the bed there. Let me get things ready. It'll just be a minute."

"One moment, doctor," the man called out as he got up from his chair. "I think I better not. I'm feeling much better."

The doctor froze, his face visibly saddened. He sank back down into his chair and leaned back with a sneer. "You probably don't trust that a quack doctor like me knows how to treat people."

Letting out a soft sigh, the man looked at the doctor with a neutral expression. "Not at all," he said. "It's rather because I believe you can do it. Let me come clean. The truth is, I came with the intention of testing your legitimacy as a doctor. But now I feel ridiculously stupid. You treated people here for almost ten years. That has more than proven your case. I only wanted to make a decision about whether or not to do something, that's all."

"But you still haven't told me—what has everyone been saying about me?" the doctor asked, still hung up on this point.

"The villagers like you of course. In the time I've been here, over a year now, I've heard them praising your virtues ad nauseam. They all hold you in high esteem. Only they don't understand why you moved away, and now that you're back, you've been acting so mysteriously that it's making people feel intimidated."

The doctor shivered hearing what the man had to say. "Is that true? Are you sure you're right about that? Even though they all know that I'm not a doctor? I don't understand . . ." He shook his head, smiling. "Oh, I can't believe it. I was scared to death, scared that people would think I'd betrayed them."

The man shifted on his feet; he had assumed a blank expression, as if apathetic toward the doctor's triumph or tribulation. "Why don't you conduct yourself as you did before, doctor? A lot of people in the village are sick.

They're in need of a doctor—a doctor like you." Venturing farther into the "clinic," he scanned the entire room, laughing quietly to himself when he spotted the patterned pillow and bedsheets behind the screen. Out of curiosity, the doctor, whose face by now no longer bore any trace of anxiety, twisted around to see what the man was looking at. When the latter sat back down, he appeared to want to say something to the doctor, but instead kept silent.

"It's a shame," the doctor said, acting like he had fallen into a vat of honey and the sweet nectar had then seeped into his veins. "I shouldn't have moved away so hastily. The truth is, the day I left, I wasn't thinking clearly. It was just a passing thought. Two days earlier, I'd realized that people were gossiping about me in the village. They knew that I was stationed at a private hospital in the nearby town, but no one knew what my position there was."

"And what was your position?" the man asked.

"I was the nursing administrator; I'm a nurse anesthetist. I'd assumed word had gotten around here that I wasn't a doctor. I don't really know how knowledgeable people are about such things. At first I tried to keep calm, thinking that no matter what, I had successfully treated the village for almost a decade. But that afternoon, I drove back from the hospital and opened the clinic at five thirty as I did every day, and then I sat there waiting. I don't know if it was just a coincidence, but no patients came in that day. It rattled me; I got so worried when I thought about how there might be patients sick in bed at home who were afraid to come and have me treat them. I waited and waited, sitting there until my legs fell asleep. By nine o'clock, when it was about time to close, I knew for sure that there weren't going to be any patients, so I got up and hobbled out front—I had pins and needles running down my legs. I went to sit on the bench in front of the house, hoping to get the blood flowing again. Auntie Yong's shop across the way was still open, and she was also sitting out front. That was another thing. Usually, Auntie Yong and I talked every day, whenever I bought things at her store. If I was having a slow day, I would cross the street and go sit with her, and we would chat. When a patient showed up, I would run back to my clinic, and then once I had finished, I would go back and we'd chat some more. It was like that for years."

"And that day she didn't chat with you?" the man asked.

"Well, I was thinking I'd go over and talk with her as usual." The doctor laughed and then continued, "How funny it all was! I stood up to cross the street, but the tingling in my legs got the better of me. It hurt to walk. It was then—right after I'd sat back down—that I noticed how strange Auntie Yong was acting. I was in the middle of massaging my toes. I don't know what was on her mind, but suddenly, she stood up and scratched her tummy sheepishly somehow, and then went back inside the shop, shut the gate, and didn't look my way again. That was the point that I knew I couldn't stay here anymore. There was no way I could stand her walking away from me for a second time. So I moved out the very next day before dawn. How could I not have been hurt? But if you compare the situation then to now, doesn't it seem odd? Aren't you curious? Why are the villagers willing to trust a fraud like me?"

"I know why," the man said. "I know very well why, but I think it's best if you don't find out. Besides the fact that it would be pointless, it might not be good for you."

It wasn't as if the doctor didn't detect the chilliness in the man's voice, but he didn't know what to make of it.

"Why don't you drop by and talk to Auntie Yong, doctor? I've heard her grumbling about wanting to see you. I'm going to say goodbye now. It seems to me you'll be able to open the clinic and welcome patients tomorrow. I'm off," the man said. He then turned and was on his way.

Once the visitor had left, the doctor put him completely out of his mind. For some minutes, the doctor sat there, feeling exceedingly pleased with his own life, and then he got up and walked out of the house, cutting a diagonal path across the road to Auntie Yong's shop. He saw her sitting on the bench out front with several others. As he approached, she quickly made room for him, and the whole group put their hands in prayer to *wai* him.

DANG'S BARBERSHOP WAS just five doors down from the grocery. Young men were constantly walking in and out, but Dang sat quietly all by himself in a barber chair, chin in hand. The men greeted him as they entered and then disappeared into the back room. It was still raining out, and the man of a certain age tiptoed along the road to avoid puddles. When he poked his head into the barbershop, Dang quickly perked up, sprouting a grin.

"How's it going, Dr. Charn?" Dang said when he walked in. "You haven't been in for ages. Is the clinic slow today?"

Dr. Charn smiled back but didn't reply. He walked over to comb his hair in front of a mirror, tilted his head left and right, and then craned his neck toward the back door to have a peek.

"I closed up around five today," he said. "You've got a good crowd here." He went to lean against the sink, crossing his arms over his chest.

"There sure is! That's why there aren't many people coming in for a haircut anymore. These guys get into fights just about every day. A few times they've even bumped into customers while they were getting their ears cleaned—you should've heard them! The sound coming out of them was barely human. The other day when Don split his eyebrow and ran over to see you, I almost died laughing. Normally, that ridiculous Don is the one stirring up trouble. He loves to get a brawl going and then back out and play the referee, whacking everyone with a cue stick, pretending to break up the fight. But that day, he hadn't come to horse around. He actually wanted a trim. So I was cutting his hair, and then his gang came running out of the back, chasing each other around with cue sticks, and they wound up smacking him right on the eyebrow." Dang pointed at his own brow, laughing. "I just cracked up. He hasn't shown his face around here since. I guess he's waiting for his eyebrow to heal."

Dr. Charn didn't react. Had it been any other time, he probably would have burst out laughing like Dang.

The barber cocked his head at Dr. Charn. "I saw. You went and talked to the doctor, didn't you? How did it go?"

"I just wanted to meet him. There was nothing more

to it," Dr. Charn said somberly. "Your doctor's going to reopen his clinic tomorrow."

"You just wanted to meet him, huh?" Dang smiled knowingly. "Don't keep it from me, Dr. Charn. I know—you wanted to test him, didn't you?"

"So what?"

"So, does he know how to treat people?"

Dr. Charn scoffed at the question. "If I say yes, you'll laugh at me, but if I say no, it'll look like I have something against him."

"Don't be so sensitive, Dr. Charn. I just asked a little question. I simply want to know if the doctor knows how to treat people."

"Didn't he treat you for almost ten years? If he couldn't do it, you'd probably be dead many times over by now."

"There, there. Just as I'd expected." Dang chuckled. "In my opinion, you shouldn't have gone and put him through whatever test. It could only make you feel worse. I'm not siding with the doctor here. I'm worried about you! You should be nice to the doctor. Otherwise don't say I didn't warn you if he doesn't share patients with you. People here, they're the only ones around, Dr. Charn. Now that we have two doctors, I don't know if there'll be enough patients for the both of you."

Dr. Charn sighed and gave Dang a half-hearted smile. "Nothing to worry about. I've already come up with a solution."

"Really? That's good. Oh, the doctor doesn't know that I have a snooker table in the back of the shop. I bet once he finds out, he's going to come over here and lecture me. He's always going around worrying about folks.

As far as I've seen, nobody takes his advice to heart. But everyone likes to be lectured by the doctor. I don't know why. It's like, when the doctor pays attention to you, it makes you look important."

"I should get going, Barber Dang. Actually, I only came to say goodbye," Dr. Charn said, moving toward the door. "Seriously, Dang, when you get a lecture from the doctor, you really feel important?"

Dang laughed. Not waiting for a proper response, Dr. Charn walked out of the shop, the barber still calling after him, "Do you want to feel important, too, doctor?"

Dr. Charn's clinic was one street over from the doctor's. He came back to find the old woman on a hunt to clean up chicken manure. She turned to him and smiled her completely toothless smile. In one hand, she held several tattered newspapers; in the other, a wet black rag. She always kept these two items at the ready for cleaning up after her chicken. Having acknowledged Dr. Charn, she turned her attention back toward the chicken, which was pecking at insects on the ground.

The old lady, the chicken's owner, was hard of hearing. To get her to understand, one had to practically yell into her ears. Once the message got through, she would reply by nodding or shaking her head; she hadn't spoken a word to anyone for years. The shed near the temple wall had been her home. She had one son, who was nearly fifty years old and small and scrawny like her. He worked odd jobs and sometimes crept up the hill behind the temple to catch wild chickens for food. Two months ago, mother and son had come to see Dr. Charn with five wild-chicken eggs in tow. The old woman's son had noticed that Dr. Charn possessed a lamp, the heat from which could be used to incubate eggs. When Dr. Charn had agreed to it, her son had left the eggs and taken off. Since that day, the semi-deaf old lady never returned to her shed again. She instead had kept a constant watch on the wild-chicken eggs, storing them in a square tin bucket. But before they had the chance to hatch, she broke three of the eggs. The chick that emerged first proved to be the strongest and pecked the other one to death, so in the end only one wild chicken survived. Once the chick was thriving and Dr. Charn could use his lamp for reading again, another problem arose: the chick had grown attached to the light and thought that the lamp was its mother. The old woman ate and slept at Dr. Charn's from then on, looking after the chicken as it snoozed during the day and hunted for insects under the lamplight at night. By this point, Dr. Charn's patients were all well accustomed to the old lady and her wild chicken.

During the entire two months she'd been living with him, Dr. Charn never thought about having a talk with the old woman. He had arranged a place for her to eat and sleep. The old lady seemed as undemanding as could be, never becoming a source of concern for him. He only spoke to her, or did his best to, when calling her for meals. Although her son never showed up at the clinic again, Dr. Charn never let the matter of the old lady and the wild chicken burden his mind. It even had a calming effect on him to see the wild chicken roaming around pecking at insects; he found it amusing to watch the woman dutifully pursuing trails of chicken droppings.

But now the matter weighed heavily on Dr. Charn. She was happy living there, tending to her chicken so that it didn't disturb his work, and she liked to serve as the clinic's makeshift security guard when he was out. But the time had come to explain to her that he was leaving. There wasn't going to be a clinic for her to watch over anymore. It wasn't going to be easy: yelling through the conversation and getting her to understand the situation so that she would move back to her old place. Getting her to hear anything at all was already such a challenge. Maybe he should go see her son. It'd probably be easier to convince him to come pick her up and take her back, but the hard part was—would he even be able to find her son? He'd heard once or twice that no one lived in the shed next to the temple anymore.

Dr. Charn sat down on a bench inside and stretched out his legs, vacantly watching the old lady and her wild chicken for some time. He tried revisiting his own situation: What if he refused to move? But he could already see how that would end. If they had to choose, how many patients would want him as their doctor? Perhaps no one would. After all, the old doctor was back. In truth, the doctor wasn't just a doctor but a hero to the people here. Dr. Charn didn't deny that the doctor was a good person, but sometimes the doctor's saintliness made him sick. He couldn't put his finger on exactly why he felt that way, so he tried to push the animosity out of his mind. A number of times, Dr. Charn readied himself to speak with the old woman, but he felt exhausted before he could even manage to get out a single word.

At nearly eleven p.m., a visitor came to see Dr. Charn. He had already closed the clinic for the night and was putting up the mosquito net for the old lady. Next to the net was the tin bucket where the wild chicken liked to sleep. The old lady was still sitting on the floor under the light, with the chicken nearby, darting about in its relentless search for insects. Dr. Charn, for his part, had still made no progress on initiating the conversation with her. Standing outside, the doctor was clutching the metal gate as he called to Dr. Charn, saying there was something he thought they ought to discuss that night.

Once inside, the doctor couldn't fight the urge to inspect the premises. What struck him first was how much the place exuded the atmosphere of a clinic. Toward the front there was a waiting area for patients; to the right was an examination room, with a hallway to the left leading toward the back of the house. Peeking underneath the swinging doors into the examination room, the doctor could see a chair and the legs of a table; these pieces of furniture were probably used for patient consultation. Outside the examination room, cardboard boxes with various medication labels were stacked on top of one another and pushed against the wall; and nearby, there was a small mosquito net, the strings from its four corners dangling, with, of all things, a square tin bucket standing next to it. The doctor eyed the old woman and the chicken, a bit disconcerted by the sight of them. Once he turned away, he saw Dr. Charn waiting on the bench, observing him. Cautiously, the doctor sat down.

"I know to some extent what's on your mind," the doctor began. "Barber Dang told me you're thinking of moving away. I don't agree with that decision at all, Dr. Charn. If you do that, you'd turn me into a selfish person who goes around interfering with other people's livelihood. I don't see why it's necessary for you to leave. I even think it'll come together nicely. Hear me out. I know that you're not working anywhere else, and therefore it's simple. You can open your clinic during the day and close at five p.m. As for me, tomorrow I'm going to go to work at the hospital as usual, and then I'll come back and open my clinic in the evening until nine p.m. See? Nothing needs to change."

Dr. Charn processed the doctor's offer impassively.

The doctor continued, "You don't have to worry about there not being patients. I promise that you won't starve to death! Please trust me when I say that everything will be just fine. Trust me, don't move anywhere. It was never my intention to cause anyone trouble."

Dr. Charn remained unstirred. But he suddenly snapped to attention once a certain haziness cleared. It hit him that he was now in the same position as all the other villagers: a recipient of the caring generosity of the saintly, universally admired doctor. He, however, didn't appreciate what was being handed to him.

"I think you best not meddle in my affairs, doctor. I really don't see why you have to be worried about me or promise to help with anything. My leaving is no major inconvenience like you think. I've moved I don't know how many times. It's no big deal. You should go. Whether or not I'm staying, it doesn't concern you."

"How could it not concern me?" The doctor knitted his brows. "I can't help but feel you're leaving on my behalf, and you shouldn't worry about that."

"No, no—it's best you leave now. If you make me say anything else, you might regret it."

"You're the most stubborn man I've ever met, Dr. Charn. I beg you—"

"All right, doctor," Dr. Charn snapped. "Fine, I won't

go anywhere. I'm going to stay right here. But let me tell you something—don't you want to know why the people here aren't put off by the fact that you're not a real doctor? It's because the villagers don't care. It's that saintliness of yours, so high and holy, that they revere. I get now what a great trade you've made for yourself. You pat the villagers on the head with your kindness, and in return you command their deference and respect. I've decided not to move, but why don't you make a somewhat bigger sacrifice for me? Move away from here again—can you do that? Because if you stay, no one's going to want to be my patient. Sacrificing for the sake of others is well within your character, isn't it? Plus you have a fancy job, no financial worries. But me, this clinic is all I have. Since I'm so needy, it seems I'm going to have to lean on you, doctor, and under these circumstances it would be quite a noble sacrifice. You do it for the villagers all the time, do you not?"

The doctor's face tensed. "Why all the sarcasm? If you're pissed off about something, just come out with it. I mean you well, really I do. But I can't do what you're asking. You know how much I love this place. Moving away was a rash decision, and I was miserable the last two years I lived in town. I was in constant contact with my landlady because I hadn't cleared out some of my furniture. I kept checking whether someone had asked to rent the place, so I'd know to come get my things. Only a few months after I moved out, someone did ask to rent it . . ."

"Oh, that was probably me," Dr. Charn said.

"Do you know what I did? I suddenly felt possessive of my clinic, very, very possessive. So I continued to rent it, never having the courage to move back. Month after month, I needlessly paid the rent . . . You can ask me to do anything, Dr. Charn, but don't make me move away again. Trust me and follow my plan."

"Of course—I knew it! I knew there was no way you'd leave. You're not worried about being surrounded by the people you love, doctor; it's just that those people are willing to bow before you and put you on a pedestal. *That's* what you aren't willing to lose. Am I right, doctor? And the way you force your damn heroic sacrifices on everyone, I see how it's a clever move—"

"Don't you talk to me that way," the doctor spat, red in the face. "I've never thought such things in my life. Who's on what pedestal?"

"But you've already gained so much. Haven't you taken a look at yourself to see how grand you've become? The people here are practically the size of ants by now! The bigger you grow, the smaller they shrink."

"If you don't shut up, I'm going to punch you in the mouth," the doctor seethed, eyeing Dr. Charn with contempt. "Do you think I don't know what kind of doctor you are? One day you go and place bets on snooker, and the next you go get drunk and mix with the unemployed rabble. All you have is a piece of paper that says you're a certified doctor—and you have the nerve to look down on me?"

"You've got all that right, doctor. I really am that way, and in truth there's more! Someone of my character shouldn't be a doctor, right? Of course, I remember now—an old woman told me that you treated her son once, and she desperately searched for a chance to repay you in some way. Do you remember how she repaid you?

It was at the temple fair. She said she gave up her front-row seat at the *likay* theater for you. To this day, she still relishes the fact you were willing to take her chair."

"If you don't shut your mouth, I swear to god I'll make you!" the doctor shouted.

"If someone of my character shouldn't be a doctor, then someone of your character *exceeds* being a doctor by a long shot, I think. But even if I don't have an elderly lady giving up her chair for me, I don't feel inferior to you. Me, I'm just an ordinary person; I'm not more or less of a human being than you or anyone else. Ha! *You know how much I love this place*," Dr. Charn said in a mocking tone. "Under the weight of your superiority, your love is also diminished to the size of an ant."

The doctor shot up from his chair. Eyes bloodshot and head cocked, he stared at Dr. Charn.

"Now, now, doctor. That's hardly a befitting expression for a saint."

The doctor moved around the coffee table, coming for Dr. Charn. At the same time, the latter noticed something beyond the gate, off to the side. He stood up to investigate, but before he took one step, the doctor's fist rammed squarely into his left eye, sending his face sideways as he fell backward onto the floor. The punch may not have been executed smoothly, but the blow did quite a number on Dr. Charn. The table creaked from the commotion, and the wild chicken started flapping its wings, fleeing to perch on top of one of the examination room's swinging doors, which then started moving back and forth wildly, causing the chicken to struggle to maintain its balance. The old woman, meanwhile, was crouched behind the mosquito net with just her head poking out, her little round eyes, their lids sagging, glued to the doctor. Dr. Charn sat up, still disoriented, the doctor's crazed taunts ringing in his ears.

"Get up, Dr. Charn! Get up! Let's go—today we're going to settle this once and for all." The doctor was agitated and getting louder. "With a doctor like you, polite conversation won't solve anything. It's got to be settled this way. Come on, fight me!"

When Dr. Charn came to his senses and regained awareness of his surroundings, the first thing he saw, looking through the doctor's legs, were people, a throng of them in the street crowding outside his gate. They stood hushed, staring silently.

The doctor quieted down when he sensed that something was off. He spun around and was met with countless pairs of gawking eyes: men, women, the elderly, even children. He froze, but the onlookers didn't budge. Dr. Charn slowly got to his feet, chuckling to himself.

"How are you going to live this down?" he whispered to the doctor. "In ten years, I'm guessing no one ever saw you get belligerent, barking at someone like this." Dr. Charn was standing behind the doctor; he would have relished seeing the expression on the saintly doctor's face then. He noticed the man was trembling, as if he were furious, yet his hands hung limply at his sides and his shoulders sagged, as if he were spent.

Eventually, the doctor turned back around. Dr. Charn could hardly believe his eyes: the doctor wasn't going to confront him but was evading the villagers' gazes. As soon as he had turned, he stared at the floor, and tears began to flow.

"Why are you doing this to me?" he asked, sniveling.

"I know you don't believe me, but I'm still going to reiterate that I love this place, love the people here. I want to stay here, and I want those people to love me back. Is that so wrong, Dr. Charn? How can I stay here if they don't love me anymore?"

"Don't you realize yet, doctor, what's slipping away from you now? It's not love. What you're losing, rather, is your pedestal."

The doctor fell silent as he listened to Dr. Charn with dismay. He wanted to object but couldn't manage a word.

"Why are you upset?" Dr. Charn continued. "Didn't you say you were never after glory? Losing it now shouldn't matter so much to you then."

The doctor shook his head, tears still running down his face. "I'm not going to listen to you. You've never meant me well—I know."

"But I've never meant you harm either. I simply think that we're equals, no one more or less than the other. I believe that you're a good person—a good person in your heart, certainly, doctor. But a laurel has sprung up on your head. It grew out of your good intentions, your generosity, out of the villagers' love and respect. But it ended up taking on a life of its own, and it's made you appear grander than your fellow humans, that's what it is, doctor. But why, why does one human being get to look down at another, and why does that other have to then look up?"

The doctor still had some fight left in him. "Even if I've got a laurel on my head like you say, what's wrong with that, when it grew out of goodness?"

"Once it's emerged, it's no different from one that came from evil," Dr. Charn fired back.

"I don't believe you, Dr. Charn. You've never had one, so how would you know they're the same?" Those were the doctor's last words before he spun on his heel and stormed off. The crowd made way for him and then watched him go.

Dr. Charn closed the gate after him, and went over to the old woman and motioned for her to get inside the mosquito net and go to bed. Then he grabbed the wild chicken, now curled up asleep on the door, put it in its tin bucket, and shut off the lights. He felt a sense of relief now that he had decided not to move away. The old lady's son might never return, and since there was nobody living there, the shed next to the temple would probably collapse soon, if it hadn't already.

THE NEXT DAY, the doctor went to work at the hospital. On his drive home, he brooded over whether to open the clinic once he got back. Self-doubt rose up inside him and brimmed over like water, and then it slowly receded again, with a struggle. His mind squirmed the entire time. If he opened the clinic and no one came, what would he do? What did people think of him now? Or was this fear an overreaction like the one before? He wanted to know if Dr. Charn had opened his clinic. If so, had any patients gone to see him? Or was he still thinking of moving away?

The doctor turned off the main street and onto a dirt road. Thick rain clouds were moving in from the east, while to the west, a gentle sun cast a warm yellow glow onto the surface of the road, which was muddy and unpleasant to look at. The sun shone on the doctor's face, but only on the bottom half, because he was sitting up tall so that his eyes were in the shade.

THE WAY OF THE MOON

IN SILENCE, MY FATHER LED ME BY THE HAND AS WE made our way along the path. He had on an enormous backpack. I didn't know what was inside, but it looked really heavy. With the full moon that night, we had no trouble seeing our way. Still, I kept a tight grip on the flashlight I'd grabbed as we'd tiptoed out the back door of the house, my father tugging at my arm. My father forbade me from turning it on, though, and I realized that if I did, my mother would instantly spot us and his plan would be ruined. I glanced back at the house, now with only my mother and little brother inside. The kitchen light was on; my mother was probably there.

"Are you worried Mama's going to find us if we use the flashlight?" I asked, already certain of his answer.

"Yes, but there's more. It's important, too—how do you feel about walking like this, without the flashlight?"

"Is it because the moon's so bright that even without the flashlight, we can see everything?" I said, glancing up at him. The moonlight was indeed very bright: I could see my father's face perfectly. Bending down, he took the flashlight from me and put it in his hulking backpack.

"For me, it's not just about being able to see. I prefer to hike by moonlight."

I didn't catch everything he said, but I knew that my father loved the moon and the way it glowed.

We walked for a long way. I tripped on tufts of grass more times than I could count and struggled on the uneven ground as I worked to keep up with my father. The ocean was getting closer; I could hear the waves. I felt that today I was fully an adult. I might have only come up to my father's waist, but I was grown enough for him to let me tag along and really do something with him.

And then we reached the sea. My father had brought us to a white-sand beach, very small and very narrow, with a knoll of scary-looking dark rocks to one side. He spread a tarp on the sand near the rocks, put his bag down, and told me to sit tight. The ocean water appeared a shadowy gray, rather spooky. The wind was blowing so strongly that I started shivering as soon as I sat down, but before long my father returned with a heap of firewood. Together we tried to get a campfire going, but it took some time for the flame to catch. In my head I kept thinking about how I had to go to school tomorrow and that my father would probably have us head back soon. I lay with my head in his lap, looking up at the sky. Ribbons of clouds glided over the moon, strand after strand. Sometimes it seemed like the moon was drifting behind stationary clouds, but then the clouds would begin moving again as before. My father picked up his harmonica and began to play, the flames casting a warm glow on his face. The melody and the crashing waves nearly blended together into one sound. I lay gazing at his long beard as it shifted back and forth in the wind, and I was lulled to sleep.

When I awoke, my father was no longer playing his harmonica. Instead, he was singing a song. I thought I'd been asleep for hours, but seeing how the moon had barely moved, it probably hadn't been very long.

"Do you have a lot of friends, Papa?" I sat up, and we started poking at the fire for fun.

"Yes, Son. Your papa's got quite a lot of friends."

"How many, Papa? Twenty?"

"Not that many. I have five dear friends."

"Oh . . . well, I have more friends than you do. I've got thirty-three! Everyone in my class, they're all my friends," I said, wanting to brag.

"But I think I've got more," he said, but I doubted it. How could five outnumber thirty-three? He continued, "I know that you don't understand, but when you're older you'll learn for yourself that many of your friends will turn into mere acquaintances, and then you'll have to go back and recount the number of friends you have left. The five friends I have, that was by my last tally."

"When was the last time you counted?"

"When I was still a young man."

"Wow! You haven't made any new friends?"

"I look for new friends all the time, but it doesn't come easily." He left it there, and I didn't say anything more, but the thought stayed with me. Wait until next year and the following year and each year after that; I was going to keep telling my father how many friends I had left.

We had been sitting there for a very long time, it seemed to me. I was actually getting nervous: my father might have forgotten that I had school tomorrow. The later it got, the brighter the moon shone. I didn't understand why the moon enchanted my father so much. He never stayed home on nights like tonight. I couldn't say whether he'd been out doing things like this during every full moon, not that we were really doing anything. We were just sitting around, but my father looked happy, like he didn't have a care in the world.

"Our house is in front of the ocean, too. Why don't you go sit on the beach there?"

"That place belongs to others. It isn't ours, Son."

"But other people go sit there, so we can, too, can't we?"

"Yes, but this place belongs to us. Isn't it better for us to come sit somewhere that's ours?"

"Ours? Is it really yours, Papa?" I was overcome with excitement. I hadn't known.

"Yes . . . mine, and yours, too. Do you feel like this beach is yours?

"I do, Papa. How long have we owned it?" I was thrilled, and my father seemed pleased to see me that way.

"We don't own it in that sense, Son; just that right now, in this moment, the beach belongs to us, that's all."

My father said those words with a straight face. I didn't like it when he'd try and trick me like that. In the past, he'd often told me, this here is ours, that there is ours, and I would fall for it and believe him every time. But sometimes, like tonight, I really did feel the same way, that this beach belonged to us, to my father and me.

My father probably noticed that I'd grown quiet, so he picked me up and put me on his lap. He cocooned me in his thick, roomy jacket, buttoning it up and leaving only my face exposed, like I was a baby kangaroo. Right away, I appreciated the cozy warmth.

It was really windy, so the flames ate through the wood quickly. The twigs had completely disappeared; only a large log remained, which probably wouldn't burn all the way through even after the whole night had passed. Sparks were swirling in the wind. My father rummaged around in his backpack for a few things: there was a can of the beer he really liked, a juice box for me, two large rolls and six tangerines. No, he hadn't purchased these items himself; he simply took from the refrigerator or the table what my mother had bought to have on hand. Only when I saw these supplies did I realize how hungry I was. My father was probably hungry, too. I slipped out of his jacket, and we finished it all off, except the beer.

My father was about as fond of beer as he was of the moon. On many occasions, my parents had fought about it. My mother said it was a waste of money, but lately she had been the one buying it, and I'd caught her drinking it a number of times when my father wasn't home. Wait until I get a bit bigger, I thought, I'm going to taste it for myself. But I'd have to sneak around both of my parents, so it wouldn't be easy.

My father got up and maneuvered the big log deeper into the flames. I was lying on my back, comfortably splayed out, my tummy and mood satisfied. He poked the fire with a stick to keep it neat, and a shower of fiery dots chased one another into the air, the wind as their vessel. I loved seeing them glimmering and glittering in the dark. But they vanished so fast. What a waste, I thought. If they had just stayed in the fire, they would have continued to glow for a long time. But if they really could return to the flames, they would no longer be the sparks I found so delightful.

"Papa, do you like the sparks that float up?" I called out to him. He was still sitting across from me, next to the log, tending to the fire.

"Of course. I've liked them for a long time. You're starting to like them, too, aren't you?" my father hollered back, smiling broadly.

"Yes, but how do we keep them in the air for longer, Papa?"

"Look at the stars in the sky. What do you think of them?" He looked up, and I did the same.

"You're right. They look just like the sparks, don't they?"

"Yes, Son, and they've been suspended up there for ages, just waiting for you to notice them." My father kept his gaze skyward.

"You're right, Papa. What a fool I've been."

For the first time in my life, I carefully studied the stars. How incredible—they looked so alive. I spotted many stars that had just begun to peek through in the busy sky; some of them little, some of them large, those bodies of light crowding one another, competing for what little empty space was left. There were more stars out tonight than I'd seen on any other night, and I'd already thought they were infinite. We were silent for some time. My father lay down on the sand, resting his head on the long log, the far end of which was burning. The flame continued to crackle, sending more sparks racing up in pursuit of each other. I still liked watching them, but I had stopped feeling that they were being wasted.

The moon had moved and was now hovering just above the ocean. My father stood up, brushed the sand off his body, and came over to sit next to me. He appeared to be wide-awake. I, on the other hand, was getting sleepy and had almost fallen back asleep several times. He sipped the rest of his beer and played the harmonica for me some more.

"Is it difficult to be a writer, Papa?"

He stopped playing. "No, Son, but not everyone can do it."

"If I love the moon like you do, can I be a writer?"

"Of course. You, my son, can surely be a writer—but the moon can't be the only thing you love. You've got to love other things as well."

"Like what?"

"You don't have to choose right now, but you must first be a person who has love inside of him."

"What are the things I have to do?"

"It's probably along the same lines as how you've learned to appreciate the sparks and the stars. In the future, I'll help guide you in the right direction."

"And when will I be able to write?"

"Why don't you try writing tomorrow? See how it goes, and we'll go from there."

"Yes, Papa, tomorrow I'll start writing."

My father got up to adjust the firewood once more and then returned to lie down next to me. I nodded off eventually, but I knew one thing: my father never slept a wink. Watching the moon, he never let his eyes rest. He must be waiting to catch it falling into the water, I thought. But even after I'd woken up, it was still floating in the sky, and even after the sun had risen, it continued to stay there suspended, glowing white like before.

MY FATHER LED me by the hand as we left through the back door. Together, we walked quietly along the path, his backpack looking like it had grown a little since last time.

"Why is it so dark tonight?" I asked as he clicked on the flashlight.

"We left a little too early today. The moon's not out yet. What did you talk about with your mama?"

"Mama gave me a blanket to bring along. She said she doesn't feel like writing me a sick note like last time." I was smiling in the dark. My father probably was, too.

THE SECOND BOOK

BOONSONG JAISAMAK MUMBLED THE ADDRESS TO THE driver and climbed into the back seat. He was holding a brown paper bag on his lap. The driver pulled the rickshaw away from the curb and pushed himself up onto the saddle, tensing his legs as he began peddling. The breeze brought with it the stink of the driver's body odor and the smell of alcohol. Boonsong quickly expelled his breath and averted his face, knowing his efforts were in vain. Eventually, he resigned himself to the situation and sighed. *This guy probably hasn't showered for three days*, he thought. *And he probably has alcohol pumping through his veins. Poor bastard.* Gradually, the rickshaw picked up speed. The driver swerved and dodged adroitly, his judgment evidently unimpaired by the inebriation. Boonsong sighed again, this time at himself, his thoughts wandering back to days gone by.

Even now, he still couldn't believe that he'd ended up a man with nothing to show for all those years. He'd given it everything he had; there was nothing more he could have given. From here on out, he wasn't going to hope, wasn't going to persevere, wasn't going to try and control his life anymore. Disappointment had ruined him beyond repair, and he couldn't bear it any longer.

The sky was overcast. The vehicles and homes passing by appeared cool on the eyes without the sun's glare. Boonsong had known this town well as a child. His family had stopped here often, parking their pickup truck to shop for household items and agricultural supplies and stock up on dried foods, before dashing off to the farm, which was in a remote area and could only be reached via back roads. The last thirty or forty years had brought many changes, leaving him with nothing he recognized. This area had developed: nice shophouses lined the streets; the roads were neatly paved. It was easy to see and to feel the progress. But the decline and deterioration lurking within him were not so apparent. They were coldly and quietly eating away at his spirit, intent on making him suffer alone. Bitterly, Boonsong reflected on his life: if fate hadn't cheated him, based on progress and protocol, he could have been the country's prime minister by now. It hadn't been unattainable or unrealistic. His current situation, on the other hand, he'd never imagined as a possibility.

Once upon a time, Boonsong had been the right-hand man to the boss who controlled the eastern region of the country. Everyone in the inner circle knew he was the guy their kingpin trusted most. Boonsong's dream of becoming editor of a local newspaper had been realized overnight, since it was in line with the boss's own agenda to have a mouthpiece. And soon the voice put out by that mouthpiece received a countrywide boost when most of the local newspapers agreed to collaborate on the founding of the Thai Regional Press Association. Boonsong had served as the body's president term after term. When he was thirty-two years old, he was elected for municipal council. Two years later, he ran for a seat in the provincial council and was elected without a hitch, given the boss's support, financial and otherwise. In terms of their rapport, he and the boss were like partners in crime, and always knew what the other was thinking. Boonsong's star had risen so high that he was above mingling with the other members in the boss's entourage. He knew full well that many of them harbored resentment toward him. It hardly bore mentioning that a number of those people had been working for the boss a lot longer and were older than him. That was just how it was, and he felt no need to waste time thinking about such things. All his various responsibilities already kept him chained to his desk, and, more importantly, he knew he still had a lot to learn and needed to lay a stronger foundation in order to eventually run for parliament.

Burned into his memory was the day that foundation, which he had believed was as solid as could be, had disintegrated as if it had been made of sand: the boss was assassinated by an associate, who then put himself in charge. The abruptness of the event caught Boonsong by surprise. He found himself cut loose, adrift. The new boss's power grew swiftly, and, improbably, his influence became even vaster than his predecessor's.

Consequently, Boonsong was left a caged mouse, scowled at with disdain. Nonetheless, he refused to give up and remained determined to make it to parliament. If he succeeded, it would mean he could truly stand on his own two feet, or so he told himself.

Before the cutoff date for registering his candidacy, a young man with an arrogant air about him asked to run alongside Boonsong. He brought nothing to the table, hoping to receive Boonsong's support and lean on whatever clout he had left. But Boonsong unceremoniously turned him away because he himself was in a place where he had to claw his own way to the shore. Not to mention his financial resources were too thin to support another candidate. And then the unimaginable happened, something that he would remember for the rest of his life: he suffered a humiliating loss in that election, while the young man pulled off a decisive victory. To this day, Boonsong could still clearly envision that rookie campaigning, how his rusted old pickup truck ran around town, clanking all the way. At one campaign event, the truck was parked under a tree, its owner standing on the roof with his feet planted in a wide stance, his hand holding a megaphone to his mouth, broadcasting his party platform. On the hood of the truck, there was a tin bucket with a paper sign that read: CAMPAIGN DONATIONS APPRECIATED. Boonsong remembered taking his wallet out and dropping in a hundred baht as a reward for the young man's determination, without it occurring to him that the money could have had such unexpectedly far-reaching consequences.

Boonsong only continued to regress. He tried one more election cycle but lost, so he went back to running for provincial council. He won by the skin of his teeth, but in the reelection he fell completely out of orbit. In the end, he failed to gain a seat even on the municipal council. At the same time, someone else became the president of the regional press association, and the handful of positions he held to enhance his social standing began to slip away, until all that remained was an editorship at a small newspaper that barely provided any income. And then came his final attempt. Boonsong swallowed his pride and went to see the new boss to ask for his support in his bid for a parliament seat. Even though he had already mentally prepared himself to be ridiculed and sneered at, he still came out emotionally obliterated. The outcome made it abundantly clear to him that he should quit politics for good.

After this string of defeats, Boonsong lived every day of his life in a kind of stasis. He let his newest wife run the newspaper and support him. His days were eaten up by spiritless gardening, reading and sitting in silence, reminiscing about the good old days, going back to the time when the concept of a boss was meaningless to him, back to his childhood of both happiness and hardship. His family had been poor, his parents farmers. When school was in session, he would stay with his uncle at the house in the rice paddies, waiting for the rice-farming season to start; only then would his parents and older sister return from working the cassava farm in another province. Once the rice season was over, they would go back to work on the cassava farm, while he would wait, counting the days until he got to join his family. Sitting around like this, waiting for time to pass, made Boonsong feel as though he were a child once more. If it were school vacation now, he would probably be preparing to leave for the cassava farm. Memories of his youth reminded him of a dream he'd had back then, a dream that had fallen by the wayside. Later on, when he'd thought he was a grown-up, he had cast it aside, thinking it childish. His hopes and dreams had become those of an adult, and they were too big and important for him to concern himself with trivial matters.

The rickshaw pulled up to the sidewalk. Boonsong looked at the small wooden street sign, recognizing the name as his destination. The letters were painted white against a blue background, and bits were missing. He got out of the rickshaw, paid the driver, glanced at the brown paper bag in his hand, and then started down the street. He counted the houses on the left-hand side one by one, each an old-fashioned wooden house on stilts, all similar to one another; and surrounding each plot, large trees grew, dense and disarrayed. He stopped in front of the seventh house. The front gate was closed, the house dead silent, with no hint of movement from within. Boonsong stepped toward it, but then paused nervously. Ever since it had first crossed his mind to do this, he had been constantly wavering, going back and forth until he felt only ambivalence. He stood in place, deliberating for the last time. Ultimately, he reminded himself that this was hardly the time to dither. He had made a firm decision several days ago, and it had cost him a considerable amount of time and energy to find himself standing in front of this house, which belonged to someone he didn't even know. But the other half of his one childhood dream, left unfulfilled, had been left behind with this person . . .

When Boonsong reached the stair landing, the front door opened. A middle-aged woman appeared wearing a dark blue sarong and a white blouse with red dots and puffy sleeves.

"Excuse me, did you use to own an old bookshop that was next door to a fertilizer store in the market?" Boonsong asked.

"A bookshop? No, not me . . . Or . . . Oh yes, my sister had a bookshop, but she leased the place to someone else ages ago."

"That must be it. I'd like to see your sister, if possible."

The woman eyed Boonsong. "What business do you have with her?"

"If your sister's home, may I come in? It will take some time to explain."

Still visibly skeptical, the woman nonetheless nodded and allowed him into the house. And at long last Boonsong came face-to-face with the person he'd been searching for. She wasn't what he had expected: she looked like she could be twenty years older than him. He could vaguely recall that he had been about fourteen years old then, and he'd guessed that she hadn't been over twenty. For the first time, it hit him how much faster women wither than men. He was fifty-two now, but the elderly woman before him appeared to be pushing seventy. Whether she would remember a minor encounter from a few decades back, he wasn't sure.

"What brings you here?" she asked Boonsong with obvious curiosity.

He didn't reply but instead took the object inside the brown paper bag out to show her. It was an old book. She barely gave it a second glance before she looked up at him, anticipating an explanation. The other woman brought him a glass of water and then sat down next to her sister.

"You probably don't remember," Boonsong began, "but I bought this book from your shop . . . let's see . . . almost forty years ago. The thing is, I bought just the one book—look." He angled the book to show the two women the spine. "Volume one, you see? This book comes in two volumes, but I only bought the first. You probably understand now. I came because I'd like to buy the second volume. I—"

"Sir, you don't have to explain further. You might as well go. The bookstore was rented out to someone else a long time ago, and we can't help you. It's best you leave," the older of the two sisters said, looking as though she'd heard enough.

"Please let me explain. From what I've gathered, I'm positive that when I bought this book, you were still running the shop."

"What do you want from us? I hate to be blunt, but do you have a screw loose? Or maybe this is some kind of scam? I just can't believe you'd come here asking for a book after forty years have passed, and from an old woman like me—I can hardly be bothered to remember things that are a hundred times more important than this! You're wasting your time. Even if it's as you say, we don't have that book or any other book for that matter. You really should go."

"Please hear me out. I'm not crazy. I have my reasons, and I didn't just show up here out of nowhere. I realize that too much time has passed, and that you don't sell books anymore. But I came because I felt there was a fifty-fifty chance that you might still have the book. No bookstore would sell only half of a two-volume set to a customer—except you. You were kind. You sold it to a boy, knowing that he wasn't a regular customer, as if you knew that that boy didn't have enough money. You were confident that he would be back to buy the second book—'Come back and get the second book soon,' I remember you saying. But . . . I didn't come back, and I know that no one besides myself would have bought the second volume, and the distributor wouldn't have been willing to take it back, so you must have held on to it yourself, just kept it around, without anyone reading it or wanting it other than me. I'm begging for your understanding and for your help thinking back a little to see if you're still in possession of that book, if you've lost it, or if you've sold it by the kilo. Try to remember—please."

The older sister looked at Boonsong in such a way as to communicate the futility of his plea. The younger one had had her gaze fixed on him from the start, as if she were on her guard and listening intently.

"Your story might be true, but I swear I don't know anything about it. Whether I sold only one book or two, it's entirely possible that I've completely forgotten about it. What I do know is that I don't have any more books. Now, will you be on your way?"

Boonsong's head sank, but he remained seated, refusing to budge. "I know you don't believe me. You think I've lost my mind. It's all right. I'd assumed it would be this way. In my life, I've never succeeded at anything. How I pity myself, myself in the past, in the present, and in the future—they all deserve pity. Before I came here, I thought, even though my life has been a complete failure, there was still something I could do. I was going to carry out one boy's dream that had never been realized.

That boy is me. I'm trying to fix my own life so that I can continue to live. But already from the start, I—"

"What do I have to say to make you leave? Let me be frank, are you insane? Look out the window—it's going to rain. The children are about to come home from school, and it won't be long before the men are back from work. You have to leave before they get back. You have to go now."

"Yes, I'll be gone, definitely. You don't have to worry about that. I'll be gone from my own life even." Boonsong put the book back inside the paper bag, got up, and left without saying goodbye. The two siblings stood in the doorway, watching him walk away into the first splatters of rain, getting lashed by the wind. The older sister breathed a sigh of relief and went back inside. The younger sister, who stayed by the door, inexplicably sprinted down the steps and started chasing after Boonsong, even as lightning struck and the rain grew heavier. She caught up with him at the top of their street.

Boonsong was astounded to see her. Blocking his way, the woman breathlessly told him, "The person who sold you the book was me. I was the one who sold that book. I need to talk to you, but not now. I've got to head back and make dinner for my family. If you take a right and keep walking, you'll see a restaurant called Boonlom Pochana. Go and wait for me there. I'll be there by seven." Then she walked stiffly away. It took a moment before Boonsong had the wherewithal to turn around and look after her. In the haze of the pouring rain, he felt like the encounter hadn't been real: in his eyes, she appeared as a blur.

The rain carried on until dark. Boonlom Pochana

was an open-air restaurant with only a roof and tables canopied by flowering plants. The employees had distributed a coil of mosquito-repellent incense under each table, which they lit and placed inside a perforated metal container. Boonsong nudged the coil under his table away with his foot so that the smoke wouldn't get in his face. There was faint background music coming out of a speaker hidden somewhere. On his table, Boonsong had a couple of plates of food, the brown paper bag, now wet and disintegrating, and a liquor bottle and three soda-water bottles, all empty. The tall glass sitting in his right hand was half-full of pale-yellow liquid. Boonsong had his left elbow on the table, his head resting in his hand. His legs were stretched out in front of him, and his eyes were closed, peeling partly open every once in a while. The next time they did so, his head jerked, and he looked at his watch. He got up to go to the bathroom, washed his face, fixed his hair, and straightened his clothes, which hadn't quite dried. When he came back, he called the waiter over to clear the table and then ordered a coffee.

The middle-aged woman closed her umbrella and leaned it against the table. She placed something in front of Boonsong and slowly lowered herself into a chair.

"I brought you the second book." The woman pushed an object wrapped in newspaper toward him. She ordered a lemon tea from the waiter and then watched Boonsong unwrap the package, studying his face in eager anticipation.

At long last, the second book was before his eyes. He stared at it in prolonged silence, then let out a deep sigh. "You really kept it. I can hardly believe it."

"I did keep it. It was just like you said this afternoon. I sold the first book to a boy who didn't come back for the second, so I had to keep it myself."

"What I meant was, why did you keep it for almost forty years?" His tone was so earnest that he sounded upset.

The woman looked at him uncertainly. "I thought you'd be happy to get the book, but you seem displeased. Why are you questioning my motives? You said so yourself that nobody was going to read the second book, nobody was going to want it. It's because no one wanted it that it's still here—that's not so strange, is it? You're the one who's strange. You failed to come back, and then after almost forty years, you show up looking for it. I'm the one who should wonder. In fact, I knew that the books had to be sold as a set. I sold you only the one because I was sure you'd be back. I knew that other shops certainly wouldn't sell you the second book alone. But you didn't come back—*I* should be the one to ask why."

Boonsong slumped back in his chair, the epitome of someone exhausted. He waved a hand and said, "All right, I'm sorry. I don't mean to be difficult. I'm in a phase where I've lost my footing, so sometimes my emotions get the better of me. Okay." He sat up straight, took a sip of coffee, and adjusted his expression. "To start, thank you for selling me the first book, even though you weren't supposed to. As a boy, I loved reading, and I dreamed of someday having my own library, like the one we had at school. But I didn't have any money; my family was poor. From my meager allowance, I skimped and saved, thinking that I'd buy a book of my own and bring it with me to the farmhouse to read during summer vacation."

"Your family farmed?"

"Yes, cassava for income and rice for ourselves. We lived in Chonburi but had a cassava farm in Rayong. Before we'd head out to the farm, my father used to stop at the market here in town to pick up some things. He would buy fertilizers and farming supplies at the store right next to your sister's bookshop."

"Yes, I know it. That store's still there. And so you bought the very first book for your dream library at my sister's shop. But why didn't you come back and buy the second?"

"I wanted to—I desperately wanted to buy the second book. After I finished reading the first, my plan was that, in two and half months, when school started again, I'd get some money to go toward school expenses, and when my father stopped in town, I'd use some of that money to buy the second book."

"So what happened? Did your father not stop here then?"

"He did, but I didn't have the money. That day he'd dropped me off at home before taking the cassava to the warehouse. You see, he'd only give me money after selling them the cassava. I did try to go find the book at the markets near our house. There was a bookstore that had the set on display, but, like you said, nobody was foolish enough to sell me the second book by itself, and I didn't have enough money after tuition to buy both."

"But you have the book now. You really didn't even need to wait so long. I think you probably know, if you couldn't find the book in stores, you could have ordered it directly from the publisher once you came up with the money, if they still had copies."

"Yes, I know, I know about all that." Boonsong looked around restlessly for the waiter and then ordered another small bottle of liquor. "That's not the problem. The problem is, I don't actually want the book."

"What?" The woman stared at him, simultaneously about to scream and burst out laughing. "You don't want it?"

"I'm sorry. I really don't want to discuss it anymore. It's pointless." The waiter mixed a drink for Boonsong and handed it to him. The woman looked fed up, so Boonsong eventually cracked her a smile. "Don't make that face. It's nothing strange, and I'm not crazy. People's desires shift all the time, you know. If at fourteen I dreamed of having a library, that doesn't mean at twenty I still had that same dream, and at thirty, well, my dreams were far different from when I was twenty! If as a child, I had wanted desperately to read a book and didn't get to read it, after some time, even if that book had appeared right in front of my face, I wouldn't have wanted to read it anymore. I'd have wanted to read a new book that's more age appropriate." He sipped his drink and sighed. "To get right to the point, the older I got, the less attainable the things I reached for became."

"What were your dreams once you became an adult?"

"What were my dreams?" Boonsong said with a sneer. "Why, I dreamed of becoming prime minister!"

The woman tried to stifle a smile and neutralize her expression as she continued listening.

Boonsong threw back his drink and poured himself another. "Go ahead. Go ahead and laugh at me all you want! If you didn't laugh, *that* would be remarkable. I can tell you the whole story. You'll fall off your chair laughing. I probably don't even have to tell you very much for you to get it. You see what kind of state I'm in. Yes—I dreamed of getting into politics, of becoming prime minister. Things were going swimmingly for a while, too. I was the boss's confidant. My future was bright; I could do anything. I'd started off small, running for municipal and then provincial councils, and then from there, parliament. And what happened? Now you can start laughing. The boss died! I was like a dog falling down the stairs, tumbling one step at a time. In the end, no one even voted for me at the municipal level. I wouldn't be so cut up about it except this rookie—you know the guy I'm talking about, the one who's speaker of the house now? Him. He was even poorer than me; he had no one backing him, no one helping him. Hmph, how could this have happened! Why aren't you laughing? Laugh! Oh, and there's more. I also owned a printing house. I had my mistress handle the accounting, and that bitch stole from me. She took so much that I didn't see the point of keeping the business, and ended up giving the whole damn thing to her. How about that?"

Boonsong kept pouring himself drink after drink, his speech starting to slur. Tense in her seat, the woman mumbled as if unconscious of her words, "Then why did you come looking for the second book?"

"The second book?" Boonsong feigned a surprised expression. "You haven't forgotten about it yet? Just let it go. Don't think about it anymore. It's all a lie anyway."

"A lie? You were lying to me?"

"Yes, I lied to you, even more to myself. Look, I'd hit rock bottom. I'd lost the will to go on, so I revived that silly little dream I'd had as a boy and tried to see it through. For one thing, I pity that poor boy. It's not like I can't remember how much he suffered, not being able to read the second book and see how it ended. And he never got to build his library. I told myself that if I could successfully follow through on this dream that had been left unresolved, I would go back and start pursuing my current dream once again."

"Well, you should be happy that you succeeded. You've found the second book. There's nothing left unresolved now."

"But it's a lie. I told you. It's all meaningless. I was lying to myself. I fooled myself, fooled you, fooled all kinds of people that it was something important, you know? I acted like getting the second book was a matter of life and death! But do you know why? I'd assumed from the beginning there was no way I'd find that book again, and if I couldn't find it, that would mean I failed, do you get it? I know you get it. It's so much easier for me to keep living life as a failure, letting each day go by—like a stray dog. But you—you had to go and actually bring me the second book, telling me to have faith. How terribly cruel. What am I supposed to do? In my situation, what could I possibly do?" Boonsong broke into bitter laughter, his body swaying. Face flushed and hair disheveled, he turned to find the waiter and shouted for more alcohol.

The woman looked at him speechless. She wasn't angry: in his current state, he could hardly keep himself in check. She thought back to the time she'd watched the shop for her sister, and, with naive faith, had sold the first book to a boy. That boy had promised that he would return to buy the second book. The memory became clearer as she called it to mind. She remembered how she had then had to buy the second book herself, so as to make her sister think that she had sold the whole set, and after that she had volunteered to watch the store for her sister every day in order to wait for the boy, and wait she did until all the unsold books from that lot had been shipped back. Bitterly, she had had to take the book home. She had kept wondering, didn't he want to know how the story ended? And then she had gone ahead and read it, even though she didn't like to read. She had read it to get even with that boy. He would never learn what became of the characters, how the story ended. He would never know—but she would, and in her head she had compared their predicaments: Who suffered more, a person who knew only the first half of a story or a person who knew only the last?

How childish, the woman thought, smiling to herself. She recalled how she had kept telling herself that she didn't want to know the backstories of the characters, had kept stamping out the urge to go look for the first book so she could read it, and had kept fooling herself that she wasn't suffering because of it. But whether that boy suffered, how could she have known? It was possible he had somehow gotten his hands on the second book and read it, and that was the reason he hadn't returned. She had vowed to put the whole ordeal behind her by hiding the book somewhere in the house out of sight. Eventually, she had completely forgotten about it, for a long, long time, until today. Suddenly that boy had returned—it was a shame the man he'd become was such a wreck. He still didn't know and didn't want to know how the story unfolded in the second book, and how it ended, because now he lacked even the willpower to better his life in some small way. His little childhood dream . . . what a shame.

As the woman sat there observing the broken man who no longer wanted anything from life, a desire reignited in her. It had been left unsatisfied for an excessively long time, and now she had the opportunity: that first book, that young girl. No matter that today she could no longer remember the contents of the second book, she could still clearly recall the desire she had had back then, the desire to know the backstories of the various characters that appeared in the second volume.

Forcing a smile, the woman eyed the two books on the table, took them in her hands, and said, "I'll help ease your mind. If you don't want the second book, I'll hold on to it again." She stood up carefully, her right hand hugging the two books to her chest and her left reaching for the umbrella. "You don't mind if I take the first book as well, do you? Since neither book is of use to you anymore . . . but they're still of use to me." She kept her gaze fixed on Boonsong as she backed away from her chair, worried that he might have a change of heart.

The woman opened her umbrella and hurried out of the restaurant. Boonsong set his glass down as he watched her walking off with the two books. It suddenly occurred to him what was happening. He scrambled to get up, knocking his chair over in the process. Scurrying after her, he yelled, garbling his words, "Give it back! Give the book back! Don't take it. I want the second book!" Several waiters rushed him and fought to extract money from his pocket as he squirmed and wrestled. They snatched his wallet, but he didn't care. He struggled to regain his balance in an attempt to chase after her but ended up falling on the sodden ground. Refusing to give up, he slipped and crawled through the mud, all the while blurting gibberish.

From a distance, he could see her walking under her umbrella toward the light of the streetlamp, passing the pole, and disappearing, once again, into the dark.

More Translated Literature
from the Feminist Press

August by Romina Paula,
translated by Jennifer Croft

La Bastarda by Trifonia Melibea Obono,
translated by Lawrence Schimel

Beijing Comrades by Bei Tong,
translated by Scott E. Myers

Chasing the King of Hearts by Hanna Krall,
translated by Philip Boehm

The Iliac Crest by Cristina Rivera Garza,
translated by Sarah Booker

Mars: Stories by Asja Bakić,
translated by Jennifer Zoble

The Naked Woman by Armonía Somers,
translated by Kit Maude

Pretty Things by Virginie Despentes,
translated by Emma Ramadan

The Restless by Gerty Dambury,
translated by Judith G. Miller

**Testo Junkie: Sex, Drugs, and Biopolitics in the
Pharmacopornographic Era** by Paul B. Preciado,
translated by Bruce Benderson

Translation as Transhumance by Mireille Gansel,
translated by Ros Schwartz

Women Without Men by Shahrnush Parsipur,
translated by Faridoun Farrokh

The Feminist Press is a nonprofit educational organization founded to amplify feminist voices. FP publishes classic and new writing from around the world, creates cutting-edge programs, and elevates silenced and marginalized voices in order to support personal transformation and social justice for all people.

See our complete list of books at
feministpress.org